Amanda Harper Paranormal Detective

Steve Higgs

&

Gemma Higgs

For strong, independent women everywhere

Contents

The elevator doors swished open with the barest whisper of noise. The young man stood waiting for it, was playing with his phone using just his right hand while in his left he hefted several bags that were shiny and new from a variety of shops. He looked up briefly and stepped over the threshold into the shiny metal box.

Just as the doors were closing a hand slithered between them and two pretty girls in their early twenties got in. They were chatting about something on TV, talking about the hunk who had his shirt off last night.

'What floor?' he asked, his hand hovering over the buttons. They were on the bottom floor anyway so whichever level they wanted the elevator would be travelling in the right direction. The Pentagon only had two levels with shops. It was one of the first indoor shopping malls built in the area, way back in the seventies. The many-floored office block attached to it stood towering over the Chatham skyline. The planners had undoubtedly expected the offices to be a draw when it was erected, but now they sat mostly empty.

'Three, please.' The prettier of the two girls replied with a throwaway smile.

He was also parked on three, so he stabbed the button with one finger as the doors began to once again slide closed.

With a small lurch, the elevator began moving. He was leaning idly against the back wall and had put his bags down so that he could use both hands on his phone. In front of him the two girls were still chatting back and forth about nothing much and one had pulled out her phone so the two of them could take a selfie. Then the elevator jerked to a halt and the lights went out. The cramped interior of the lift was split by a scream from one of the girls, an involuntary reaction but one that caused him to jump more than the lights going out had.

A second or so later the lights came back on and the lift started moving again.

'Oh, my God. What was that?' One girl asked of the other.

'I don't know, but I didn't like it.' she wailed in return.

'It was probably just a power outage.' he interjected, trying to sound authoritative and knowledgeable. Both girls turned slightly to look at him, maybe waiting for him to expand on his statement but he had nothing else he could think of to say.

They turned back away from him and the girl with the phone lifted it once more to try taking the selfie again. Then she screamed a scream that would echo in the man's head for years to come. She let go of her phone just as the elevator jerked to a stop and pinged its arrival at their floor. The doors swished open as the girl's phone hit the lino. She screamed again and ran out of the elevator, bouncing off the still opening doors in her haste to escape. Her friend followed closely behind.

'Your phone?' The man called after them, wondering what the hell was going on. He jammed a foot up against the right-hand door to stop it from closing and bent down to pick up the phone. As he turned it over and saw the screen his soul froze.

The girl had managed to snap the first selfie when the lights had gone out and there, between their heads and right next to him was the shape of a person. It was caught in motion and it was blurry, but it was undeniably the outline of the figure of a person in the lift with them when the lights were out. The lift pinged again, and the doors tried to close, shoving against his foot so that he had to increase the weight on it to keep it in place.

What was he seeing? He needed to show this to someone. The police? Or maybe the Ghostbusters? He could feel his hair standing on end. Staring at the screen on the phone, the lift pinged again and he realised he needed to move, go and find the two girls or something. He would send himself the photograph first though. He turned to get his shopping from the floor where he had placed it.

It was no longer there.

A few hours after the incident in Chatham and completely oblivious to it I was boarding a plane home. I looked back at the last thirty-six hours. Like all weekend city breaks it had passed in a blur, leaving my memory trying to connect all that had happened into a coherent sequence. My date for the weekend was a man I knew almost nothing about but had arrested a few days ago on suspicion of murder and then arranged for his release less than twenty-four hours later. His name was Brett Barker. He owned the Barker Steel Mill in Dartford, Kent and was a single, attractive, athletic multi-millionaire. My name is Amanda Harper. I am a police officer working for Kent police, but I already quit that job a couple of weeks ago in favour of a career as a private investigator. That statement, however, fails to capture the truth of my new job. I think I will leave it at that for now though as this bit is about the ridiculously delicious hunk I am salivating about.

Brett had approached me a few days before I arrested him and expressed his desire to see me socially. He was quite charming, and he had a confident nature that bordered on being arrogant but never went that far. He had shown a touch of nervousness when he asked me to come to Paris for the weekend and that had been what had convinced me to go. Had he been certain I was going to say yes, then I would not have done.

We flew first class, the first time I had ever done that but clearly it was the only way he travelled anywhere. He had been intending to fly his helicopter, but the weather predictions had been ominous, and the plane was safer.

When we boarded the plane yesterday morning, I was acutely aware that I had not yet been on a date with him, or even kissed him, and now I was planning to spend the night away with him in the penthouse of the Ritz, in the centre of Paris. He was being a perfect gentleman and had not tried to so much as hold my hand, but all men are more or less the same, so I set some ground rules and explained that I would not be sleeping with him that night. He took the news very well as if that was entirely expected and thoughts of getting into my knickers could not have been further from his mind. He explained that he had booked the penthouse because it came with three separate bedrooms, each with an en-suite bathroom and that I would have complete privacy whenever I wanted it.

Halfway through the first evening, I had almost changed my mind about the sleeping arrangements though. I was being swept off my feet. Being with him was how I imagined it would be to be famous, but without all the unwanted attention. Everywhere we went, he was greeted like an old friend. We were given a private tour of the Louvre, we took a helicopter tour above Paris as the predicted storm had not come to pass, and had eaten at the fanciest restaurants I had ever seen, let alone been in. Obviously, he would not let me pay for anything. After dinner, I had most of a bottle of champagne in me and I was starting to wonder what he looked like naked.

I don't make a habit of one-night stands, in fact, I abhor them and have only had two in my life, many years ago and best forgotten. This would not be a one-night stand though, I told myself, as I was planning to see him again and again and again if there were any more dates like this to be had. Instead, this would be having sex on the first date; something else I advocated against, but boy was he looking tempting now.

As we got in the lift to go up to the top floor, I slid my hand into his. It was the first time we had touched apart from when he charmingly offered me his hand to get out of the Rolls Royce we were travelling around Paris in. As the lift doors closed and we were thankfully alone, I turned into him, looped my left hand behind his head and pulled him down into a kiss. I had been just very slightly concerned that he was gay because he had not made a single suggestive comment or move on me and that had never happened before, but my worries were instantly alleviated as his tongue gently slipped between my lips and the kiss deepened.

We were still kissing ten seconds later when the lift binged to announce our arrival. Neither one of us broke the kiss though until someone coughed politely. The lift had stopped before it reached the penthouse suite level to let someone else on. As Brett opened his eyes and saw our audience, he quickly broke the kiss off and stood up straight again. In the doorway, were a cute older couple in their late seventies, dressed for dinner and holding hands. Brett said something to them in French that I could not follow and they both laughed.

The man waved a hand and replied but they made no attempt to get in the lift with us. The doors closed once more, and we continued up the last bit to the top floor.

Brett did not kiss me again but kept hold of my hand and led me to the room. As we crossed the elegantly styled lobby, he let go of my hand to retrieve the key from inside his jacket. Stood waiting beside him, I was having a tough mental debate with the sensible, rational version of myself that knew no good could come of sleeping with him this early in our relationship and the utter whore persona that wanted to whisper that the dress he had bought me to wear tonight really didn't allow for the person inside to also wear knickers. They were still arguing when he opened the door and let me inside and had come to no conclusion by the time the door was shut, and we were alone.

Thankfully, I suppose, Brett decided for me.

'Goodnight, Amanda.' he said, taking my hand and kissing it. 'I have work to do but will see you in the morning.'

Dammit.

I bid him goodnight and went to my room, hurrying lest I lose my final drop of willpower and throw myself at him. I got undressed, hoping he might come and knock on my door, and fell asleep wondering if I should go and knock on his.

That was last night. I had woken alone with a dry mouth and a dull ache in my head from the overindulged champagne. I had showered and dressed and found Brett sitting at a desk in the main room inspecting a complicated spreadsheet of numbers. Steel futures he assured me. I did not know what that meant.

He ordered breakfast up to the room and took me on a boat down the Seine to a place that sold champagne by the case and then to a gallery and then to lunch. The day disappeared and before I knew it, we were back at the airport.

The flight back from Paris was seventy minutes; barely enough time to get comfortable in the enormous, luxury leather chair/beds in first class. The cabin crew offered me champagne again, which this time I declined. I did not have to drive when we landed as he had sent a car to collect me from my flat the previous day, but I had drunk enough last night and I felt that my evening might be best spent at the gym. Secretly I was worried/hopeful that I might be seen naked in the not too distant future and felt a need to get some squats and cardio in.

I had packed only a carry-on bag to avoid the baggage queue, but I now had a Louis Vuitton suitcase that he had supplied to make sure the Versace dress he bought me to wear to the Opera last night would get home safely. Somehow though the super-rich don't need to worry about carry-on limits, so I had not had to check my bag anyway.

I could get used to this.

He kissed me lightly goodbye outside the terminal where the same car and driver that had collected me was once again waiting to take me home.

Brett Barker. What a revelation. Gentleman, millionaire and... lover?

The following morning, I awoke to an alarm which I had reluctantly set last night to go off at half past five and only hit the snooze button twice before I accepted the inevitable and forced myself out of bed. I had told myself that I needed to keep up my gym hours and I was actually feeling quite motivated as I swung my bag over my shoulder and left my flat.

At the gym in town though my motivation had abandoned me. The weights were mocking me from their stand. Why the hell are the small weights all pastel colours anyway? I don't need them to be pink for me to know that they are the ones I might be able to lift. I ignored their taunts and climbed onto an elliptical trainer where I spent twenty minutes sweating, grunting and groaning. Next to me had been an overweight man with a beard who had his machine on the minimum resistance setting and was barely even elevating his pulse. He had tried to talk to me – a regular gym hazard, so I had indicated my headphones and made out like I could not hear him. When I grew bored of the motion I switched to a treadmill. Pounding away, perspiration gathering in my bra, I daydreamed about Brett. His handsome face and light stubble grazing against the soft skin of my face, gently irritating the edge of my lips as we kissed. In my head, the kissing was getting more passionate, his hands were on my skin and digging into my hips. I could feel his... I let out a squeal as my right foot caught the stationary edge of the treadmill and I was flung off the machine to land painfully on the carpet tile.

Heads popped up around the gym. I was such a klutz. I had a friction burn to my left knee where it had hit the short carpet tile. Guys were rushing over to help me. I got up quickly, so I could wave them off. I was fine, just clumsy and distracted by thoughts of Brett getting naked for me.

By nine o'clock I was sitting at my desk with my bum cheeks already sore from the kettlebell squats I had forced myself to perform before I left the gym. My second cup of tea was cooling next to my mouse mat and I was idly working out how many hours I had left in the Police. I had quit my job a week ago, or slightly more than that now. I worked out that I had eleven shifts left. That was all. It would be ten by the time I finished today. I had been doing this job since I was twenty-one. What had I got out of it? I wanted to say not a lot, but I suppose the honest answer was that I had learned lots of life skills and I felt ready for my next job.

My next job, of course, was working with Tempest Michaels at the Blue Moon Investigation Agency. It had been my idea. I had approached him for the job rather than responding to a job advert as there was no advertised post. I couldn't work out what to make of Tempest, or how I felt about him. It was all fairly moot now as I was semi-officially dating Brett and quite happy about it, but I could not deny the fleeting interest. Tempest was good looking. Not as good looking as Brett, but few were. He was polite, funny and engaging and I found that I liked spending time with him. I had thought he was single but then went to his house early one morning to find a woman there who had clearly spent the night. He was attracted to me, he had let that slip, but had failed to make any kind of move. Anyway, we were both seeing other people it seemed.

Working at an investigation agency probably sounds quite glamourous, evoking images of Sam Spade and black and white movies where the lady detective is resourceful and tough as nails while wearing silk stockings. Well, the reality is a little different and most especially at the Blue Moon Investigation Agency where what we investigate is paranormal crimes. That sounds stupid, doesn't it? Tempest came to it by accident. There was a mess up with his first business advert and suddenly he had clients calling with crazy cases where they believed they were being targeted by a witch or haunted by a ghost or whatever. He solved each case by finding the perfectly rational explanation for the situation they were experiencing and got to charge them for it. You may think it sounds like he is conning the people involved, but they are queuing up and begging him to take their cases.

'Hey, girl. Where have you been all weekend? I sent you messages and snapchats and you didn't reply to any of them. And I know you read them because the iPhone told me.' The voice was coming from Patience Woods, a fellow police officer who was just arriving to sit at the desk next to mine. She was late. Again. We had been friends for about five years since she transferred to Maidstone from Chatham. She was currently stood with her arms crossed and was glaring down at me.

She had a good glare.

Patience is a plus size girl with boobs bigger than my head and a whole lot of junk in her trunk. Her default setting was loud, which right now meant that eighty percent of the office could hear her and were subsequently covering the mouthpiece of their headsets, so the person at the other end would not also hear her. She has more attitude than anyone I have ever met and did not care what anyone thought about her or it.

She dropped a three-pack of Krispy Kreme doughnuts on her desk and lowered herself into the chair. There was only one left in the pack, her lips were glistening with powdered sugar and as I watched, the last bite of dough-nut number two went into her mouth. She didn't break eye contact once. I felt a bead of sweat roll onto my collar.

'Good morning, Patience. How are you?'

'Don't you try that Disney Princess, white girl, butter wouldn't melt rubbish with me. Where the hell have you been?'

'I was in Paris.' There was no point in avoiding the conversation. She would get it out of me soon enough.

11

'Paris? What's in Paris?' she asked.

'Well, there is the Louvre, the Arc de Triumph, several...'

'Nuh-uh. You know what I meant. I sat next to you all last week and you never once mentioned that you were going to Paris for the weekend. So, something changed.

'I was on a date.' I conceded.

'A date?'

'Yes.'

'In Paris?'

'Yes.'

'With a man?'

'Yes.'

'Well, you better start spillin', girl. I need to hear all about your shag-fest weekend.' Patience instructed while taking a gulp of coffee and reaching for her final breakfast dough-nut.

I took a sip of my tea and from behind my mug quietly admitted that there had been no sex. Patience's eyes nearly popped out of her head with shock and I knew I was in for a grilling. Thankfully, at the same moment, Sergeant Butterworth looked up from his desk.

'Do you mind, Patience?' asked Sergeant Butterworth. 'Some of us are trying to work. I believe that if you turn on your computer there will be work for you to do also.'

She fixed him with a look, her eyes bugging out at him like she could not believe that he had the audacity to interrupt her conversation.

'Excuse me? Did you just interrupt me? Do you have no manners at all?' Sergeant Butterworth was now out of his chair and coming across the office.

'Patience, I need you to do some work.' he said as he approached her work area. 'I shouldn't have to have a fight with you every day just to get you to do your job.'

Patience leaned forward a little in her chair and indicated with her head that he should come closer. He came forward another step and leaned down.

Patience hissed. 'We are having a very private and personal conversation about Amanda's vagina. Would you like to pull up your chair and join the conversation? Do you feel that you and your vagina can give us some insight as well?'

His face turned purple and he opened his mouth to respond but Patience wasn't done yet.

'It's hard for us girls here, surrounded by dicks all day. Sometimes we need lady chats and we shouldn't have to feel bad about that. I should be able to talk about my period and the awful cramps I'm getting any time I like without being made to feel bad about it. If you got a problem with that maybe I should talk to HR.'

As Sergeant Butterworth skulked angrily back to his desk Patience chuckled to herself. 'See, girl? All you have to say is period or vagina and men run away terrified. Now, let's get back to your broken vagina.'

'Patience, my vagina isn't broken.' I replied, my voice distinctly more hushed than hers.

'The hell it isn't. Why else would you spend a weekend in Paris, on a date and get no dick?'

'I spent a pleasant weekend with a gentleman, Patience. Such men still exist.'

'Oh. So, he's gay then?'

'No... At least I am pretty sure he is straight. There was plenty of passionate kissing and there was something very hard digging into my hip while we did it.'

'Hold on. You spent a weekend in Paris in the same hotel room and you did not have sex. How do you manage that?'

'We had separate bedrooms.' I answered.

'You had... hold on, what kind of hotel room has more than one bedroom?' Patience was staring at me now, her mouth a quizzical hole in her face.

'Um. The penthouse.' I said quietly.

'The penthouse!' she shrieked. 'OMFG! Who were you with?' Everyone in the office turned to look at us. Sergeant Butterworth's head looked like it was about to explode.

'Do you remember I told you about Brett Barker?' She immediately turned to her computer screen, booted it into life and typed his name into a search engine. 'Well, he asked me to go to Paris with him, so I went.' As I finished speaking his face appeared on her screen.

'Babe. Your new dick is rich. And when I say rich, I mean Kanye West style rich.' The picture on her screen was a good one that showed just how handsome Brett really was. 'Girl, that man in fine. How did you not get stuck in the dicksand this weekend?'

Just then, the Superintendent walked into the room and with a quick, 'Oops.' Patience put on her headset and made it look like she was working.

Thankfully, we were busy then, and I could avoid further interrogation for the rest of the morning.

I heard a text ping through on my phone about half an hour before I was due to take my lunch. I ignored it until my break time came around but pulled my phone from my bag as I stood up to head to the canteen. Patience and I had different lunch break times most days, so I would be able to put off telling her about Brett for a bit longer yet. There wasn't really anything to tell. Apart from that he is gorgeous, ridiculously rich, incredibly well-mannered... I could go on, but I was trying to ignore that he was literally perfect.

The text message was from Tempest to tell me that he had a case he didn't have time for right now and to ask if I wanted to investigate it. He had forwarded me the email from the prospective client, so I switched to my emails to see what it was.

This would be my first case.

The client was the manager of the Pentagon Shopping Centre in Chatham. I knew it well. It was looking a little tired and worn but then Chatham was not really a place one went shopping unless you already lived there, and the indoor area, which was probably quite a draw forty years ago was now losing ground to bigger, brighter indoor shopping areas within an easy driving distance. He reported that he had a ghost living in his elevators. There was a poor-quality picture attached that showed two girls illuminated in the flash of the camera and a man standing behind them. Each had a startled expression, but the focus of the photo was the blurry, indistinct shape next to the man. It looked like a ghost if one was willing to believe in such things, of course. I could see through it, so I had to admit that it had a certain ethereal aspect. The client's email went on to say that several shoppers had suffered frights as the elevator they were travelling in lost power. The lights would go out and, in most cases, the elevator stopped moving, but only for a second or

16

so. Shoppers had reported that their possessions, mostly shopping bags full of new purchases had gone missing and several had reported that they had felt a draft or had felt something touch them or brush past them in the confines of the elevator. Then there was the picture captured by the two girls.

So, I had an unexplained mystery that the client was willing to pay us to solve. It was damaging his sales, he claimed, and the shareholders were squeezing his nuts to get the punters back in and the problem resolved before the Christmas rush started in a few short weeks.

I emailed back to Tempest, telling him that I would take the case and would go directly to the Pentagon when I finished my shift this evening. In the meantime, I would contact the client and arrange for him to meet me because it would be after shopping hours when I got there.

I ate the salad I had brought with me for my lunch and drank a glass of milk. My lunch break was nearly over so I used the facilities and went back to my desk just as Patience was getting up to take her break.

She made it clear that I still needed to spill the beans on my weekend but hustled off to get her lunch, leaving me to settle back behind my desk. Today the pair of us were dealing with converting calls into dispatching uniforms in response. It was often tedious, and it was not what I was usually assigned to do, but in the dying days of my career with the Police, it was what they had given me. I slipped my headset on again and the afternoon drifted away, absorbed by myriad minor incidents.

It got quiet around three o'clock, so I pushed my chair back a bit and stretched without getting up.

Patience swivelled in her chair to face me. 'So?' she asked.

'There really isn't much to tell.' I started.

17

'Don't give me that. You spent the weekend in Paris with a multi-millionaire Adonis. There has to be something to tell and if there isn't something to tell then you need to tell me what the heck is wrong with you.' Patience had fixed me with a look that made it clear I wasn't going to get away without telling her all about it. I opened my mouth to speak but she was already talking again. 'That man is fine with capital letters. F – I – N – E. If he had taken me to Paris for the weekend, I would have ridden him like a pony on a carousel. That boy would be ruined for all other women for eternity. That's how good sex with me is, girl.'

I stared at her, slightly scared and very much in awe of her self-confidence. Maybe she was right. Was I stupid to have resisted sleeping with him? Had he expected me to and through not fulfilling my end of the bargain had I now ruined any chance of a second date? My mind slowly started to drift, filled with thoughts of Brett naked. I was willing to bet that sex with Brett would be good. Maybe good. I was ready to bet that he knew what to do with a woman.

Suddenly Patience's voice cut through my fantasy. 'Girl, are you even listening to me? I know that look. You're thinking about sex with him right now, aren't you? You have that look in your eye and a stupid grin on your face.' I shook my head and cursed myself silently.

Patience had crossed her arms and was glaring at me. 'If there was no sex then tell me about the romance. I am single and need to hear that romance still exists for someone.'

I conceded and spent the next twenty minutes describing the hotel, the opera, the first-class seats on the plane, the first-class treatment everywhere we went and how he had been such an absolute gentleman all weekend. She was amazed that he went to the trouble of opening doors for me, shocked and envious that he had bought me a dress that was so expensive it didn't even have a price tag and had then bought

Louis Vuitton luggage, so I could get it home, and she was utterly confused with how I hadn't thrown myself at him when we had kissed passionately in the elevator. I had shrugged and said that it was too soon to be falling into bed.

Then she asked when I was seeing him again and I didn't have an answer. Should I text him? Thus far all the pursuing had been done by him. Was that fair? Would he welcome an invitation from me? Did I then invite him to my flat and make him dinner? I certainly couldn't stretch to a night at the opera with champagne. What if he turned up in a Bentley or a Lamborghini? It would get stolen in seconds outside my place in Maidstone.

'Patience?'

'Yes, Honey?'

'How long do I wait before I text him?'

'Girl you don't need to text him. Wait for him to text you.'

'Why is that?'

'Why? Girl, how is it that a woman with an ass like yours is so dumb about men still? He spent all that money, he wined and dined you and treated you like a queen because he wants to get at that ass. Until you give it up you don't have to do anything. After that, then maybe you got to call him or do things for him occasionally. Right now, though, that boy is yours. Make him work for it.'

I mulled that over.

'How long since you last saw him?' Patience asked rhetorically then answered her own question before I could speak. 'A few hours, right? You saw him yesterday. Don't you go looking all pathetic and needy by calling him just because he is hot and rich.'

'Okay. Okay.'

'You promise now?'

'Yes, Patience. I promise that I will not call.' She seemed satisfied finally. 'For how long?' I asked.

This prompted another lecture about being the one that is chased rather than the one chasing. It went on for a while, interrupted only by us having to actually do our jobs. Patience was single as well and I wondered if her stance on approaching men or putting herself into a relationship was holding her back from changing her relationship status. I kept my mouth shut on that subject though.

The Pentagon Shopping Centre, Chatham. Monday, October 18th 1924hrs

I had contacted the shopping centre manager during my afternoon coffee break and arranged for him to meet me after my shift finished. I didn't tell him I had to wait to finish work of course as I was representing the Blue Moon Investigation Agency and had changed into my usual clothes before I left the station. As far as he knew, I had been on other casework until this evening and this was the earliest I could get to him.

The shops were all shut, and the building was locked up at this time of day, so we had agreed to meet at a service entrance on The Brook, the road that runs between the Pentagon and the County Courts. I must have driven or walked past it hundreds of times but had never once noticed it was there. Looking for it though I had spotted it immediately and the client, Mr. Miller, met me outside as I pulled up.

'Am I alright to park here?' I asked, half out of the car. I couldn't be sure it was the client, so it could be a security guy coming to usher me away.

'Amanda Harper?' he asked.

'Yes. Good evening. Are you Martin Miller?' I offered him my business card, Tempest had provided a box of them last week.

'Yes. Good evening. Thank you for being on time.' I had agreed to get there by half past seven, so I was a few minutes early but had not been sure where the service entrance door was and had allowed some time for circling.

I locked the car and followed him inside, pulling my notebook from my bag as I went. The corridors were darkened but not dark, only minimal lighting was on at this time of day. He told me we were heading to his

21

office and that it overlooked the shopping centre, but we could have been going anywhere. The maze of corridors was vast and the route we took was intersected several times. He knew where he was going, but I would need him to escort me back to my car when I was finished here, or I would never find it.

We came to a lift. We had been talking as we walked, although the corridor was narrow, and I was walking behind him with him talking over his shoulder. He was a thoroughly average Caucasian man, by which I mean that he had no outstanding characteristics by which one could describe him. He was wearing a cheap but functional and new looking suit over his average frame. He was about my height, but my boots had a short heel, so he was roughly five feet eleven inches tall. His hair was brown, his eyes were brown, his complexion was clear and free of any trace of a suntan. He had told me that he had been the manager of the shopping centre for eight years and that it was rarely eventful or exciting. I had to steer him onto the subject of the spooky elevator he had reported, for fear he might ramble on about his job and the shopping centre for hours.

As we got into the lift, he finally started telling me about it. 'We have eight banks of two lifts here. Five of which service the shopping centre and the car park. The remaining three service just the car park. There has never been a problem with any of them until two weeks ago apart from the odd breakdown.'

'What date was the first reported problem?' I asked, pen poised.

'I have it all diarised in my office. We are nearly there.' He answered. Sure enough, the lift pinged and stopped at the second floor. We exited onto a corridor running perpendicular to the lift and turned right. His office was the second door on the left. He opened it with a key.

Inside was just as drab as the outside. There clearly wasn't much budget for decorating or improving any of the functional areas. The wall opposite the door was one large window which looked down onto the central atrium in the middle of the shopping centre. Looking down at the shops I worked out that we must be above Wilkinson's. Odd that I had never noticed the window from the other side before. The area looked very different at night and devoid of people. I felt a little voyeuristic as if I was peeking inside someone's house when they were not there.

'Here it is.' Martin announced holding up a piece of paper. 'I made a copy for you.' It showed the events in a chronological order and recorded which lift the event had occurred in, whether anything was taken, and what the shopper reported had happened.

'There are forty-seven reports from four different lifts, Martin. Did you shut any of the lifts at any point?' I asked.

He drew my attention to a map of the shopping centre on the wall to my right. 'The lifts are colour coded. The first event occurred in the rightmost orange lift on Wednesday 6th at about three o'clock. A pair of old ladies reported that their shopping had been taken, that the lights had gone out etcetera. I saw them myself actually because they were harassing security and making quite a fuss. We called the Police in the end, who came and took a statement, but they left it at that and I dismissed it, assuming they had just put their shopping down somewhere. Then it happened again the next day and twice more the day after that. I decommissioned the lift at that point and had the maintenance team check it out. I figured if no one went in it for a while the problem would cease.'

'But it didn't.'

'No. It didn't. I have two engineers that are responsible for the lifts and the escalators among other things. They checked the lift out and said there was nothing wrong with it. They both reported that they felt cold when they were inside it though. I went into it and couldn't feel anything.' He paused then as if remembering something. 'Sorry, would you like a cup of tea or something?' he asked. 'I totally forgot my manners.'

'No. Thank you, Martin.'

'Are you sure? I am having one.' I shook my head as he moved to turn on the kettle which sat on a small table next to his desk.

'You were telling me about the lifts.' I prompted, rather than wait for him to finish making his beverage.

Well, the orange bank of lifts was out of commission but the next day we had the same problem in the blue bank.' He indicated where the blue lifts were on the map. It was at the northernmost end of the complex where it exited onto the bottom end of Military Road and The Brook. On the Saturday morning, the lift opened, and six lads spilled out screaming and yelling. They were in their early twenties or late teens and convinced there had been something in the lift with them. Something had touched one of them. We had seven more incidents that day, so I shut that lift down as well.'

I was scribbling notes furiously. He waited for me to finish. 'Then what?' I asked.

'Then it was Sunday and there were two more incidents that morning. At that point, I shut down all the lifts but that lasted about thirty minutes as apparently, I am not allowed to stay open if there are no lifts. There are stairs going to the upper carpark floors but too many persons with mobility restrictions to make that a viable access route. I thought about closing the whole centre but got quite a few threats from store owners, so

24

I had to abandon that idea.' He seemed a bit lost for direction. 'So, the attacks have continued, and everyone is looking for me to solve the problem. Visitors have decreased by forty percent and I doubt I will keep my job long if I cannot sort this out.'

'I need to see the lifts please.'

'Which ones?'

'All of them.'

Martin nodded and led me out of the office. We took a long winding walk around the shopping centre using torchlight in places to illuminate the dark corners. This took a good while and there was no power to the lifts at this time of day so all I could do was look at the closed doors. I gave up before we got to the ones that served only the carpark.

'Are the lifts all the same make?' I asked as we headed back to my car.

'Oh. I don't know the answer to that question.'

'Who would?'

'The service engineers, Charlie and Jack. They will be in tomorrow if you want to come back and talk to them then. I can arrange for you to be shown the lifts then as well, although I suppose you can just go and look at them yourself at that point.'

I got their full names and told Martin I would be back by four o'clock the following day. I was working a shift until three o'clock, so that was the earliest I could return. He had led me back to my car by a completely different route, but we had been on the ground floor of the complex, not the second floor where his office was. When he had opened a door and street light from outside had flooded in, I had been surprised. We were right by my car though, so I bid him goodnight and plipped my car open.

Then I thought of something and called out to him before he could get back inside and shut the door.

'I need to be informed whenever there are any other incidents.'

'Or. Err, of course. I can do that. Or I can get my head of security, Steve Brooms to do so. Is that okay?'

'Yes. Please pass him my card,' I produced a new one from my pocket, 'and have him call me. Also, I need a list of what was stolen. Do you have that already?'

'Yes. Of course, the Police have it already but do not appear to be doing anything with the information.' I rolled my eyes. The poor police have plenty to be getting on with and this was petty crime that sounded more like lost shopping when one listened to the explanation. I opted to stay silent on that thought though. 'Can you email it across to me please?'

'I will do it before I go home tonight.' He promised. I nodded my thanks and bid him goodbye again.

Driving home, I went through what I knew. I wanted to find the answer to this case without needing to involve Tempest. He seemed to just eat these cases up, finding the answer as if it was obvious all along. This was my first case though and I needed to prove that I could do this to myself as much as to him. He was so relaxed and laid back that he would think nothing of helping me to work out what was going on.

What I had was a series of odd and unexplained thefts when I boiled it down. If I ignored the selfie with the ghost in it, the reports all said that the lift had lost power, a presence was felt in the lift and shopping bags had gone missing.

But what about the mist like figure in the selfie?

26

My phone rang loudly in the confined space of my car and I almost wet myself. I punched the button on my steering wheel to connect the hands free. 'Hello?'

'Amanda?' It was Brett's voice. The sound of it made my pulse quicken which surprised me.

'Good evening, Brett. How are you?' Was that too formal? Did I sound standoffish?

'Very well, thank you, Amanda. I wanted to see when you were free this week. I had hoped I might entice you into joining me for dinner.'

My pulse skipped again. Goodness, was I that into him? 'I, um...' What was wrong with me? 'I believe I am free Thursday night if that works for you.'

'Thursday? Yes, I can make that work. Are you okay with Vietnamese food?'

'Err, we are not going to Vietnam for it, are we?' I was joking but also slightly worried that he might have something dramatic planned.

'No.' he laughed. 'But there will be a little car ride to get there. Can I pick you up at eight?'

'Sure thing. Do I need to dress up?' I was mildly concerned that we might be eating at Buckingham Palace with the Royal family and we were eating Vietnamese food because they were hosting the Vietnamese Ambassador.

'No Babe. Ordinary going to a restaurant clothes will suffice. No trips to the opera, no private museum tours.'

'Okay. It sounds nice. I will see you then.'

'I need your address. I don't know where you live.'

'Of course. I will text it to you. I am driving at the moment.'

Dammit, did I really want him seeing where I live?

'Okay. Well, I will see you Thursday then.' He said.

'Yes. Thursday.' There was an awkward silence then as neither of us hung up. 'Okay, bye then.' I said, trying to make it sound natural and cool, like I wasn't secretly mega-excited about seeing him again. I clicked off just as he was saying goodbye to me.

At the Pentagon with Patience. Tuesday, 19th October 1611hrs

My shift today had been like many others in that it had started too early and was mostly boring. I took calls about nothing exciting at any point and was happy when it was over. I had let slip to Patience that I was going to the Pentagon to look into the ghostly elevator case and she insisted in tagging along with me.

We both finished at 3 o'clock, changed out of our uniforms and took my car rather than pay twice for parking. On the way there, Patience had asked me more about the case.

'The Pentagon Centre manager believes he has a ghost. Or at least he believes he has something odd happening with his lifts. People get in, the lights go out, the lift stops and when the power comes back on several of them have claimed that they felt a presence in the lift with them. Two girls managed to snap a selfie. Here.' I said offering her my phone. 'The first picture you come to should be the one.'

'Whoa! Jesus, Mary, and Joseph.' Patience blurted from the passenger seat. 'That's a ghost, girl.'

'I highly doubt it.'

She fixed me with a stare. 'Girl I know a ghost when I see one. My great aunt Rita was a medium.'

'Nevertheless, I believe there will be a more ordinary explanation for the image and for the reports people have made.' Quite what that explanation might be I had not the faintest idea yet.

'What else have they said?' she asked.

'There have been reports of shopping going missing. That is something that feels incongruous.'

'What kind of shopping?'

'Hmm?'

'You know, was it bags of groceries or was it fashion wear? If it was fine shoes, then the ghost is bound to be a woman.'

'I haven't been able to read that bit of detail yet.'

'I bet it was. I bet the ghost is a young woman struck down in her prime wearing fine clothes. Ooh! I bet she was killed by her jealous boyfriend because she was flirting with another man and now she haunts the Pentagon because he pushed her down the elevator shaft.' Patience was creating a whole story arc for her ghost. I had no idea she had this much imagination.

'Anyway, I am going to visit the two maintenance engineers and ask them to show me the lift shafts and grill them about the lifts themselves. I also want to ride in the lifts and see if anything happens.'

'Are you crazy? There is a ghost in a lift and you want to get in the lift and close the doors?'

'It will be fine, Patience. There is not going to be a ghost haunting the lifts in Chatham.'

'How do you know that?'

'If you were a ghost would you not pick somewhere a little nicer than the Pentagon to spend the rest of your undead existence?'

She appeared to be mulling that over. 'It is a little skanky, I suppose.'

Chatham was all of that.

The traffic from Maidstone to Chatham was moving slow. I had shot up Bluebell Hill swiftly enough but the ride down the Maidstone road into Chatham was clogged with traffic backed up behind temporary traffic lights where someone had seen the need to dig a hole in the road. It had not been there yesterday. After much stopping and starting, we eventually got through the lights and our pace picked up again. The final mile into Chatham town centre is always sticky with so much traffic funnelling into a tight space and a poorly organised one-way system, but it continued to move, and we finally pulled in to park the car at five minutes to four.

'Are you hungry?' Patience asked as I fed coins into the ticket machine. 'I'm hungry. I might get me a sandwich. You want a sandwich?'

'I need to catch the maintenance guys before they finish for the day. I need to do that first, but no, I don't think I want to get food here. I have a meal waiting at home.'

'This is why you are lean, girl. You can resist the hunger,' Patience observed. 'Let's go see your maintenance men. Then maybe I'll get me a sandwich after.'

I had called Martin Miller from the car, so he was expecting us. I probably could have parked back where I had met him last night, but I planned to check out the lifts myself once we were finished behind the scenes, so it made more sense to park in the main car park. We were on the ground floor, so I had not needed to use the lift to access the main shopping area. There was a staff entrance to the Pentagon management and service area next to Sainsbury's supermarket in the far corner of the centre from where I had entered. Martin advised that there was an intercom on the wall and that the security guard at the other end of it would be expecting us.

Getting to it proved harder than expected though: Patience was easily distracted.

'Hey, Amanda girl. Look at these fine shoes.' Patience had come to a halt in front of a store window. 'That new man of yours would love to see you in these.'

They were six-inch-high slut heels with a one-inch clear platform on the bottom. I was not convinced I could walk in them but then I was also not sure that walking was their purpose. 'I cannot wear those, Patience. They scream "Hooker" at a loud volume. I do not own an outfit that they would go with.'

'Well, that's fine, girl. Ann Summers is right next door.'

'Thanks, Patience. I am not really an Ann Summers girl.'

'You've got a new dick to impress now girl, so maybe you ought to rethink your attitude. I am an expert in Ann Summers. Let's go get some new panties, or do you think your new dick is into things that are a little naughtier?

I would tell myself that I am not a prude but the idea of something *a little naughtier* terrified me.

'Thank you, Patience, but I don't think Brett and I are there yet. Maybe another time when we have been on more than one date.' I needed to get Patience off this subject.

'The element of surprise, girl. He thinks you're a sweet little lady – then Bam! You whip off your dress and show him your crotchless panties and nipple tassels. Always works for me. Men love that stuff.'

Now I really had to stop the conversation. The mental image projecting itself uninvited in my brain was not something I could handle. 'I really need to get to the maintenance guys.' I replied, ignoring her demands to go into the store. I was trying to get her moving in the hope she would give up on the idea of dressing me like I was auditioning for an adult movie.

'You're all Miss Business today. Let's go see your men. Then we can shop.'

'Would you rather stay here? I shouldn't be too long. You can get some food and do some shopping.' I was beginning to regret bringing Patience along. I wanted to solve the case, not buy underwear. Patience looked like she was weighing up her decision, but she elected to tag along with me despite the pull of hot food.

I found the intercom, got buzzed through and was met inside by a security guy who explained that he would escort us to the maintenance guys. The security chap was called Karl. He introduced himself over his shoulder as he walked ahead of us through the same maze of narrow corridors I had been in yesterday. He was fifty pounds overweight, huffing and puffing from the effort of walking. Quite what his role might be I did not want to ask but since all a thief would have to do to evade him was walk quickly, he was probably the man they had watching the cameras. Watching them with one hand in a bag of crisps probably.

A minute later and perhaps a dozen or more turns through the maze, Patience and I were both thoroughly lost again but we arrived at a door which had maintenance room written on the outside. It was not locked, and inside were two men in their early fifties, both sitting on polyethylene chairs, one blue, one orange arranged either side of a small, dirty, round, Formica-topped table. They had half-finished mugs of tea on the table and were playing cards. The mugs were dirty, the cards were dirty and the men themselves did not look exactly clean. The walls were adorned with posters and pictures of naked girls. Calendars, pages from girly magazines and the odd faded page three pin-up covered most of the available wall space. I had been in places like this before and it no longer bothered me, their leering stares were not winning them any points though.

I knew their names to be Charles Spencer and Jack Benson as Martin had provided me a brief background on the two men by email yesterday. Security guard Karl left us with them and closed the door on his way out.

'Damn, it smells like arse in here?' Patience said. She was right, but I had elected to ignore the fact that someone had recently farted rather than lead with it.

Reassuring myself that I had tissues in my pocket to clean my skin, I crossed the room with my hand extended. 'Amanda Harper.' I said as I shook their hands in turn. 'This is my colleague Patience Woods. So, which of you is Jack?'

'I'm Jack.' said Jack helpfully.

'Then that makes you, Charles.' I said to the other chap by way of confirmation. He nodded but did not speak.

Jack was the spokesperson for the pair. 'Mr. Miller told us to expect you. You're here to catch the ghost then?'

'Damn right.' said Patience from behind me.

'I am here to investigate the unusual activity, yes.' I replied. 'Mr. Miller said that you have inspected the lifts. What can you tell me about them please?'

Jack picked up his dirty mug and drained the last of the liquid inside it. Setting it aside, he pushed his chair back slightly and turned to face me.

There was nowhere for Patience and me to sit, but I was glad of that as everywhere was filthy. He scratched his stubble, working out what to say. Then he launched into a long rambling statement about how the lifts had been fitted as part of the original installation back in the mid-seventies. He and Charlie had both landed jobs at that time, having both recently finished apprenticeships. They had been taken on cheap because they were young, and he had a good moan about how their wages had barely gone up since. The lifts had been refitted twice, once in the very early nineties and again earlier this year. They had done most of the refitting work themselves, shutting down one lift bank at a time. I asked what the refit involved, and he explained that the most recent refit had been a complete overhaul that involved replacing the cables, gearing, and controls – they had not done that work, instead it had been contracted out, and the lift interiors, doors, and lighting had all been replaced with new items – this is what they had done. The work had taken six months so far and had earned them some overtime hours as much of it was conducted when the shopping centre was closed. They had six lifts banks completed and two still to go. He explained which ones were yet to be tackled. I matched that to the map in my head – they were two of the lifts that had not reported any ghost attacks yet. Two of the six they had refitted also had no reports of attack though, so the correlation was unreliable.

'Can you show me the difference please?' I asked. I wanted to see everything as I could not yet tell what would be significant and what would not.

Just then Charles shifted in his seat and farted. Loudly. He looked utterly unashamed at his flatulence, but with Patience and I staring at him he did have the common sense to apologise.

'Sorry. I have a bit of gas.'

'You always have a bit of gas.' grumped Jack.

'Man, what you have is a lack of manners.' Patience said heading for the door. 'I will be outside.' I had to agree and found myself backing away also. It stank like garlic sausage.

'The lifts please, Jack.' I said on my way to the door. 'I need to see the insides and I need to see the lift shafts and the machinery that works them.' I was using my cop voice now. The one that insisted on compliance.

Jack was getting up as I was going out the door, thankful to be able to breathe slightly cleaner air. As the door started to swing shut, I heard another, even louder fart coming from inside the room and a chuckle from Charles.

Why is it men never seem to grow out of finding farts funny?

We did not have to go very far to get a look at the gubbins that made the lifts work. Just around the corner was a lift bank which, of course, we had approached from the rear.

'Which lift back is this?' I asked.

'Green. The ones near the toilets at the south exit. I knew which ones he meant. They only went between the first and second floor and had not yet recorded an incident. There was not a whole load to look at. The shaft itself was completely bricked in. A locked door, for which Charles produced a key, then led inside the base of the shaft. I peered inside. The two lifts were both moving above us, but I was in no danger as the area in which it would descend was inaccessible behind a steel barrier.

I asked a few questions about the machinery, what sort of problems they had to fix, but I did not really have a line of enquiry to follow. I decided that I did not need to see the hidden workings of the other lifts at this time, if ever, so my next move was going to be to see the lifts as the customers did. Something odd was happening but I still had no idea what was causing it or how it was that shopping had gone missing.

I had one last question for Jack and Charles though. 'Mr. Miller told me that you inspected the lifts after the incidents. What did you find?'

'Nothing.' said Charles immediately. 'The lifts were operating perfectly within tolerance.'

'No electrical faults. Nothing to explain why they would have stopped working or have the lights go out.' chipped in Jack.

'I reckon they have been making it up.' said Charles. 'The first person lost their shopping and made up a story. Then it caught on.'

I thanked them for their time and asked Jack to escort us back to the shops. The two men were convincing in their belief that there was nothing wrong with the lifts. It had been one theory, actually my only theory so far, that the lifts were just suffering from breakdowns and the rest of the ghost story was just embellishment followed by others repeating the tale and pretending they had been involved. It seemed less likely now that there were so many cases involving so many different and unrelated people.

Back out in the shops, the air was sweeter, but I felt a need to visit the ladies just so that I could clean my hands properly and freshen up. Patience agreed.

A few minutes later and feeling far cleaner, Patience was on the hunt for food again. 'Girl, my tummy is empty. I need a sandwich now,' she claimed as we exited the facilities.

There were no food places inside the Pentagon. It seemed odd now that I thought about it, especially compared with modern malls that all have a food court crammed with eating options, but Sandwich Palace was just outside the Pentagon on the upper north side.

'I'm gonna get me the party platter.' Patience said more to herself than to me. I sat in a booth and had her get me a diet coke. While she was queuing at the counter, I took out my phone and sent a text to Brett. I had forgotten to give him my address. Okay, that is not strictly true. I had tussled with whether to give him the address for my crappy flat near the station or to pretend I lived on the other side of the river in the nice apartments. In the end, I accepted that I would not get away with it for very long and would struggle to explain later why I had felt the need for my subterfuge. I doubted he cared at all about where I lived. He had enough money for both of us, or in fact, for most of the population of Maidstone, plus he knew what I did for a living, so he knew roughly what I earned.

Once I sent the text, I gave Tempest a quick call.

'Hi, Amanda.' he answered. 'How are you today?' He was always so polite and engaging.

'Fine, thank you, Tempest. I am in Chatham looking into the ghost at the Pentagon.'

'Oh. How is that going?'

'Nothing to report yet. I am just eliminating leads and getting a feel for what might be going on.' I really wanted to solve this for myself. Not for the sake of my own ego, or so that I could prove to Tempest that he was right to hire me, but for myself. I needed to prove to myself that I could do this.

'Well, if you need to use any equipment just come and get it from the office. Or if you need an extra pair of hands at any point just let me know.'

'How is the Klown case going?' I asked. Tempest had been hired to investigate the disappearance of a man, but it was an odd case because the man was not actually missing. He had joined a weird Klown cult that had sprung up recently. They were responsible for a lot of graffiti across the county that claimed the *Klowns are coming*. They also appeared to be behind some odd stalker type behaviour where several girls had been followed home at night by scary looking men in clown outfits. Nothing more sinister than that had occurred though until a few days ago when a girl was attacked with a knife. She had lived but was badly cut on her abdomen. It was scary stuff, but the man Tempest was engaged to find was answering his phone and refusing to come home. The client was the man's sister, who assured Tempest that he was in danger and needed to be rescued.

'I am not sure there is a case.' he replied. 'I tracked him down and spoke with him, but since he does not want to come home and is doing nothing criminal, I don't see what there is that I can do. I am considering giving the client her money back.'

'Have you spoken with her?'

'Not today. When we spoke yesterday, she once again implored me to bring him home at any cost. That would be kidnap though. He has every right to join a Klown cult and wear odd clothing if he wishes to.'

We talked for a few minutes more and I promised to keep him updated on the case as it progressed. As I disconnected, Patience was arriving back at the booth with a giant sandwich sticking out of her mouth. She shoved the coke at me and pulled the bread away ripping a large chunk off with her teeth.

'Damn this is good,' she said between chews. The party platter consisted of a selection of sandwiches plus a bucket of fries. I wondered if she planned to eat the whole thing. It was designed for a family to share. Generally, I did not allow myself to indulge in such fatty treats, but it did smell good and my stomach gave a little growl as I considered maybe having one piece.

'Are you sharing?' I asked, lifting my right hand to snag a sandwich from the platter.

She scowled at me from across the table. 'You said you didn't want anything.'

'Hey, Hotstuff.' came a familiar voice. I turned to see the huge form of Big Ben blocking out the sunlight. He had just come through the door uncharacteristically alone. Big Ben usually had a woman with him, or so it seemed. Admittedly, I usually saw him with Tempest, but listening to the stories about Big Ben and the inordinate amount of shagging he does, my senses told me he had to be in the company of a woman pretty much all the time.

'Hello, Benjamin.' I replied pleasantly. I turned to introduce Patience only to find her with her mouth open and a piece of lettuce hanging out. She looked like a dog staring at an especially tasty string of sausages.

'Hi. I'm Big Ben.' Big Ben said, introducing himself. He was smiling at Patience and she was completely bewitched. I had to admit it was a smile that was nice to look at. Big Ben was good for looking at if nothing else. He fell firmly into the category of man-candy at six feet and seven inches of solid toned muscle topped with an unfairly handsome face. I would never allow myself to be attracted to him though because I knew about his social habits: He went through women at the rate of one or more a day. I would have to fill Patience in on this later.

40

'Murgh murrf,' said Patience. She had managed to find enough self-presence to swallow the piece of sandwich she had been eating but coherent speech was still evading her.

'This is Patience,' I explained.

'Patience,' Big Ben repeated. 'That is something I could do with more of in my life. Maybe you can help me out with that.' he said hitting her with a huge smile. I rolled my eyes.

Big Ben slid in next to her, forcing her to scooch along a bit to allow him enough space. Smiling amiably still, he wiggled his eyebrows and selected a French fry.

'Help yourself,' Patience invited him, finally finding her voice. She leaned forward at that point, pulling down her top slightly to reveal even more cleavage. It was a slick and clearly well-practised move.

'Hmmm... I see you have both the Italian Chicken, made from breast meat and the giant smoked chicken barbeque sandwich, a personal favourite of mine, which is made from thigh.' Big Ben claimed, his voice now taking on a husky edge. 'Of course, I really like the dark meat.' He said locking eyes with Patience. The usually sassy woman, who bossed men around and totally owned her own life just sat there and swallowed nervously.

OMG I was starting to feel uncomfortable. They were doing verbal foreplay in front of me.

'Patience?' I called across the table to get her attention.

'Hmmm?' I got in reply with a single raised eyebrow. It was as if she had forgotten I was there.

'I need to go and check on the lifts. Are you coming, or shall I leave you here to eat?'

'You go,' she said, still looking at Big Ben. 'I'll catch up.'

That would probably work better for me anyway. Minus Patience, I could check out the lifts without her trying to drag me into any shops. I put my phone away, picked up my diet coke and left her with Big Ben. I bid them both goodbye but neither one looked in my direction.

Back inside the Pentagon, I checked every one of the lifts in turn. Both lifts on each bank. I could find nothing out of the ordinary in any of them. The two that had not been refitted this year stood out because they were old and grubby and graffitied. They seemed to be a little bigger than the others, which struck me as odd, but I assumed that the new panels to be fitted inside were thicker or something. There seemed to be little more I could gain by staring at the inside of the lifts. I had ridden each one up and down with no ghosts jumping out at me and no loss of power at any point.

I sent a text to Patience as an hour has passed and I had not heard from her. I was planning to leave now. A few seconds later a text message pinged back to tell me Patience had already left Chatham with Big Ben. She had called me three times before giving up. Sure enough, there were missed calls on my phone when I looked properly. I guess the signal didn't get through while I was in the lift or something. Her text said she would see me in the morning and she felt no need to expand on that. I wasn't sure what I should write back. Good luck? Hope he is hung like a donkey? I elected to just leave her alone and hope she did not feel the need to regale me with any stories tomorrow.

I checked my watch: It was 1757hrs. The Pentagon shops had already closed and the centre itself would be shutting its doors very soon. I walked back to my car and set off to interview some of the people that had reported the ghost attacks and missing shopping. Martin Miller had furnished me with a list of names last night. I had then found addresses for the names while I was in work today. Most of them were local. The nearest was a man who had been the second to report that his shopping had gone missing. He was walking distance from where I was but for speed and efficiency, I drove to his house with a plan to drive onwards from there anyway.

Tyreke Franklin was a Jamaican man in his late fifties. He answered the door in house slippers, grey hopsack trousers held up with bright red braces and a white vest. He had a thick head of dreadlocks going down his back to almost touch his trousers and he had a great smile with a single gold tooth in place of his top right incisor. He invited me in almost before I had introduced myself.

The house had a trace of marijuana about it, the sweet smell lingering in the fabric of the soft furnishings. I wanted to speak with as many people as I could, or perhaps as many as it proved necessary to form a consistent picture of the incidents, so I ignored the obvious smell, declined his offer of a drink and pushed the conversation forward.

'You reported the incident on Friday 8th. This was at,' I checked my notes, 'four o'clock. Yes?'

'That is correct, my dear.' he said, his voice a rumbling baritone.

'Can you please describe the event? Give me as much detail as you can please.'

I listened as he started to describe going to the roof to have a smoke. The pentagon is the highest structure around that is easily accessed and he liked to go up there and enjoy the view. On the way back down the lift had stopped. The lights went out at the same time, but it was only for a second or so. He thought nothing of it until he had arrived on the ground floor and noticed that his bag was missing. He had just bought a new pair of Nike trainers in Foot Locker and was going home. He assumed he had left them on the roof and had just imagined bringing them into the lift with him, but he could not find them there either. It was only then that he remembered hearing something about odd occurrences at the Pentagon on the local news the night before. He told me that he had wondered who he should tell, but then while he was standing next to the lift, he had spotted a pair of Police officers and waved to them. He told them the tale but could see one smiling to the other while he took notes. Then they asked him how much weed he had on him and confiscated the tiny bit he had left with a warning.

I wondered who the cops had been as this was pretty dodgy behaviour. I did not ask though. Instead, I pressed Mr. Franklin for more information. Asked him what else he remembered. There was nothing though. I thanked him for his time and thanked him again when he wished me good luck in my quest to solve the case.

I moved on to the next address. Two hours later I had visited six more victims, all of whom had similar tales to tell. There were a couple of differences though. One was a pretty girl called Poppy who had taken her little brother shopping to get a present for their mother's birthday. Poppy was seventeen, her baby brother, as she called him was fifteen and had a black eye. The black eye it transpired had been delivered by Poppy in the lift when the lights went out and someone had grabbed her left boob. She thought it was her brother and had whacked him in the face. Only when she saw that the shopping was gone, and he continued to deny any wrong doing did she concede that it might not have been him after all. Then she said something else that sparked my interest. She said that the lift had an odd smell to it. Like someone had been in there with food. I asked her to describe the smell but neither she nor her brother could pin down what it was they had been smelling. The best they could do was label it as something meaty. My interest dwindled – it was probably nothing more than the previous occupant getting in the lift with their lunch. Walking away from their house, I wondered if the smell meant anything, but I had learned that the ghost liked to cop a feel. My guess would have been that it was a man behind this anyway, but it seemed more certain now.

I would have ignored the remark about the smell had I not heard it again from a different victim that had lost their shopping on a different day in a different lift. Alison Daniels had not had her boobs fondled but she said the lift stunk and she almost got out again when she stepped in and gagged on the smell. Her description was of very heavy garlic but somehow not. I filed the information away, wondering if I could add two and two together to arrive at four, or if this was a red herring that I should ignore.

I was tired when I got home. Too tired to cook anyway, so dinner was a fishfinger sandwich using bread I had in the freezer. I made a few notes about the case on an A4 pad I had to hand but when my eyes started to droop, I went with them and fell into bed.

The alarm went off at 0600hrs, drilling a hole into my brain until I found the off switch. My shift was the last in this particular sequence. Usually, the pattern was four earlies, then two off then four lates then two off ad infinitum, but in my notice period I had unused holiday to take so was using it up by chipping days off. I had three days off after this one. Buoyed by that thought I swung my legs off the bed and headed to the shower.

As I lathered my hair with the last dregs of my favourite Aussie shampoo, I made a mental note to add it to my shopping list and considered what I needed to do about the Pentagon ghost today. I wanted to get some cameras and see if I got lucky with them but would not have enough time after work to collect them from Tempest in Rochester and get them to the Pentagon in Chatham unless I arranged it with Martin and I did not want anyone to know that I was doing it. Maybe I could get Tempest's LGBT, cross-dressing assistant Jane/James to drop it off on his/her way home. He/She lived near Maidstone somewhere, so it felt possible.

While I was in the shower, I decided I ought to perform some downstairs maintenance before my date with Brett. Just in case... I had no intention of him seeing any of it yet, but equally, there seemed no harm in paying some attention to detail. I also shaved my legs and then went the whole hog, scrubbing my body with my favourite Molton Brown exfoliator. I left the shower, dried myself then liberally applied a matching Molton Brown moisturiser all over. I felt good and that was probably all that mattered.

I blasted my hair with the dryer and went into finishing touches. A tinted moisturiser, a swipe of mascara, nothing else. I didn't feel the need

46

for a huge effort at work. I had no interest in the men there and honestly could not care what they thought about my appearance.

I threw on skinny jeans and a jumper, added a pair of boots and headed for the door. I would change into uniform once I got to the station.

On my way there I called the Blue Moon office from the car. It was Jane/James that answered. How did I address him/her if he/she did not say who was speaking? I decided to always go with James if I did not know.

'Blue Moon Investigations, Jane speaking. How may I help you?' That made things easier. He had decided to be a girl today.

'Hi, Jane. I need to use some of the camera equipment, the really small ones, but I cannot get there today to collect them. Will you be able to drop them off at the station on your way home later?'

'Err, yeah. I don't see why not. How many do you want?'

'How many do we have?' I asked.

'Six, I think. I will check. Shall I just bring them all?'

How many did I need? I have eight banks of two lifts, so I would have to put whatever we had into some of the lifts – probably the ones with the most frequent occurrences and hope for the best. 'Yes, that would be great. Thank you. You can ask for me at the front desk but if they say I am unavailable you can just leave them there for me.'

'No problem. See you later.'

I pulled into the carpark behind the station where the sky was threatening to rain. There was moisture on the breeze and a dangerously dark sky in every direction. I was down to work the dispatch desk again today so it hardly mattered.

Inside though, once I was in my uniform, I found that I had been switched out and would be on the streets instead.

'Hey, girl.' called Patience as she crossed the room juggling a set of car keys. 'Dannermann and Jones got injured and are on the desk. You and I get to go out for the day.' She was looking rosy and chipper. Why was she looking so pleased with herself?

OMG she actually slept with Big Ben last night!

'Did you shag Big Ben?' I said a little louder than I ought to. Everyone in the room turned to look at us.

'Damn, girl. Can you say it a little louder?'

'Sorry.' I blushed. 'You did though, didn't you?' Our voices were hushed now so others could not hear what we were saying, and they had gone back to whatever they were doing.

'A lady never tells.' she said demurely.

'Yes... but you're a total slut.' I pointed out politely.

'Girl, that boy is fine. What is wrong with you that you didn't already hit that? How come you're always around all these fine-ass men and you never get any dick? I wasted no time. I rode him like a carousel.'

I couldn't deny that Big Ben was incredibly attractive, but like David Beckham, the illusion was broken when he opened his mouth.

I needed to move Patience onto a new subject before I got a full breakdown of last night while we stood in the office. What I said was,

'Never mind that. How did you wangle getting the two of us on patrol together?'

She checked around to see if anyone was listening then leaned in close like she had something secret to tell me. 'I didn't. They put you on with that Hardacre doofus, so I switched the names around on the board. We need to get out of here quickly before someone notices.'

'Patience...' I started but then realised that I didn't care. I was no longer chasing a career here. I had nine shifts left including this one, so the old me that would have toed the line and done as I should have, was rebelling and up for some fun.

'Let's go.' I said snatching the keys from her hand.

'Hey! I'm driving.' she yelled after me as I headed for the door. The hell she was. Patience was a terrible driver. It was one of the primary reasons she was on the dispatch desk.

Outside the rain had started, it was a steady drizzle that threatened to get worse. I held the key fob in the air and watched to see which car would react. A silver Ford Fiesta plipped its lights, so I dashed across to it and dived in before I could get too wet. Seconds later, Patience plopped into the passenger seat. If she really wanted to drive the car, she was showing no sign.

I started the car and pulled out into traffic. We had nowhere that dispatch was trying to send us yet, so we were supposed to take up a position on the outskirts of Maidstone town, close to the motorway. The inactivity was unlikely to last long, but now that I was not trapped at the station, I wondered if I could get away with whizzing over to the Blue Moon office in Rochester. I could grab the cameras and then later, if we were quiet, I could whizz to Chatham and put them in.

Yup, I was going for it. The best route at this time of day would be up Bluebell Hill and then down through Borstal to the back of Rochester Castle. It wouldn't take long.

I knew Patience well enough to know that she was waiting for me to ask her about Big Ben. I also knew that if I ignored the subject or danced around trying to avoid it, she would get ratty.

I gave in and asked her. 'Soooo... about last night?'

'Girl I am exhausted! That man is like the energiser bunny. He kept going for hours. We did it in positions I've not seen before and trust me I've done a few. My Hoo-ha is still recovering this morning. I feel like I have been riding a horse all night.'

I could not say I was surprised. Ben had apparently slept with a lot of women and had a lot of random, emotionless sex. What did surprise me was the look on Patience's face. 'Patience, do you like Ben?'

'Honey, I don't know Ben, but I like his body. And his dick.' she whispered. 'So that's enough for me to give him a second go.'

'Patience, I hate to break it to you, but Big Ben doesn't do second goes. He's a one night only kind of man from what I know. I don't want him to break your heart.'

Patience burst out laughing. 'Honey, don't you worry about me. This has nothing to do with my heart and the only thing likely to get broken is my Hoo-ha.'

The conversation about her Hoo-ha and Big Ben's amazing dick lasted most of the fourteen-minute drive to Rochester. The roads were clear, and people tend to just get out of the way of a police car. I parked next to Tempest's Porsche and went through the bottom door that led up to his office. There was conversation coming from the office, I could hear Tempest and Jane discussing something. They stopped though as they heard boots on the stairs and a head peered around the edge of the half-open top door.

'Good morning, Amanda.' Tempest said. As always, he was well dressed in casual, but new office wear. A pair of Ralph Lauren tan jeans with a white Gant shirt. He was a good-looking guy that looked after himself.

Behind me, Patience had clearly spotted him as I heard her whisper, 'Hot damn.' under her breath.

'Hi, Tempest. I was put on patrol, so I have come to collect the cameras instead of having Jane drop them off.'

'Cameras?' he asked. Clearly, Jane had not told him I planned to use them.

'Yes.' said Jane, invisible behind the door until Patience and I reached the top of the stairs. 'Amanda is using them to catch the ghost at the Pentagon.'

'Well, I hope I can capture it in action. Trouble is there are more lifts than we have cameras.'

'Any theory about what is happening there?' Tempest asked.

'Not yet. At least I don't think I have anything tangible. The Pentagon manager is a little odd, there is something off about him. But so far, all I know is that there is something odd going on.'

Patience cleared her throat. We had been ignoring her.

'I'm terribly sorry. That was rude of us.' Tempest said thrusting out his hand for her to shake. He was always so terribly British. 'I'm Tempest Michaels. How do you do?'

'Patience Woods.' she replied, letting his hand go. 'I thought I heard two men when I was coming up the stairs.'

'Hi, I'm Jane.' said Jane standing up.

'Whoa.' Patience was gawping at Jane. It was the effect she had on most people when they discovered the tall, but petite, pretty, blond girl was, in fact, a man. Today Jane was wearing a wool dress and Ugg boots between which were a pair of patterned tights. It was all in hues of burgundy. Around her neck was a scarf that was mostly cream, but it was big enough to hang down over her flat chest to disguise it. 'Are you a dude?' she asked.

'Not today, no. I have two personalities fighting for dominance, one male, one female...' I had heard the explanation a few times before. I was surprised that Jane did not get bored reciting it.

Patience was looking Jane up and down, inspecting her. Jane finished explaining that she awoke each morning gender neutral and let her mood dictate which underwear drawer she opened.

'So, you have a cock?' Patience asked. I rolled my eyes and walked away. Tempest had gone across the room to where he kept the equipment such as cameras and listening equipment. He also had night vision goggles and some other gear as well as a few weapons – nothing illegal and it seemed to stay put in the cupboard, so I made no comment about it.

Behind me, Patience had a list of questions to ask Jane, so I busied myself helping Tempest get the cameras out of the box they were in. He was checking each one turned on and that they had a battery charge.

'Six of them. Unless you want to take the infrared as well, in which case I have another two which will make it eight. The infrared will not pick up much unless it is dark though.' He explained.

'Hmmm, that might work. The lights are reported to go out whenever there is an incident. The lights go out, the lift stops for a couple of seconds and then they come back on. Something is happening when the lights are out as several people have reported their shopping bags have gone missing.'

'So, we have a thieving ghost riding an elevator?' Tempest said, amusement in his voice. Tempest knew with utter conviction that there was always a rational explanation to the odd cases he investigated.

'That is what I intend to find out.' I replied, meaning it.

I knew how the cameras worked. They were tiny things, barely bigger than a thumbnail and would run for most of a day on a single charge. Like tiny webcams, their output could be linked to a single computer anywhere and watched remotely with all feeds on one screen.

'You need anything else?' Tempest asked.

'No. I don't think so.'

'Well, if you come up with something you do need just call me. I will bring it. I do not have a lot going on here today.'

'No case?' I enquired. 'It sounded like you were discussing one when Patience and I were coming up the stairs.'

'A banshee. Jane had a very convincing email from Rita Underworth. A banshee living in her bedroom closet, keeping her awake at night, should she be worried about it sucking out her lifeforce when she did sleep. Could I help, etcetera?'

'It sounds just like your kind of case.'

'Exactly. So, I made a phone call and discovered that Rita Underworth is nine years old. I spoke with her mother and the banshee is the old boiler which makes noises in the night as water gurgles through it. Jane and I were just laughing about it when you turned up because I almost drove to the address instead of calling first.'

My radio squawked from its position clipped to my lapel. Dispatch had a job for us. I took the box of cameras, thanked Tempest for his help and told him I expected to be able to wrap the case up in a couple of days. Patience was still asking Jane about her junk and where she put it so that it didn't show up if she was wearing tight jeans. I shoved her towards the door. We needed to go.

The call we responded to was a domestic disturbance. Fortunately, it was this side of Maidstone and we got there in just a few minutes – before dispatch enquired where we had been anyway. Dealing with it, arresting the lady of the house when she continued to be violent even after we arrived, took up the rest of the morning and it was after lunch before we were free to consider going to the Pentagon to put the cameras in. That was what we did though.

I parked the squad car right next to the doors that led from the car park to the shopping centre. Why circle looking for a spot when I had my own park anywhere-I-like device? Patience asked what we were doing, so I explained as best I could that I was going to put the tiny cameras on the ceiling of the eight lifts that had suffered the most frequently reported incidents.

I considered telling Martin Miller what we were doing but decided against it. If no one knew, then there was no chance of a warning getting back to the person or persons behind this.

'Alright, ladies.' Came a voice from behind us. I groaned internally. It was not unusual for young lads to think it acceptable to make inappropriate comments or suggestions to female police officers. However, it happened in Chatham every single time as if it were a sport or as if the idiots get taught it in a class at the school they are most likely playing truant from.

As I turned around to face the voice, I grabbed Patience's arm. Her eyes were already bugging out, she hated being disrespected.

'Young man I suggest you be on your way before I take an interest in you.' I would rather warn him and leave both he and his gaggle of spotty friends to annoy someone else, than get distracted by dealing with him. I could tell by his leering smile it would not work.

'Hear that, fellas? The stripper doesn't want to play today. Come on love, show us yer tits.' There was a chorus of "Yeahs!" and "Yay, tits!" from the moronic cohort stood behind him.

I moved towards him. He darted back a few feet. I still had the cameras and laptop stuffed in a box under one arm and would need to put it down to grab him.

'I bet those tits are smashing. I can see how big they are even with the body armour on.' He was still laughing at me, but it vanished soon enough as Patience snatched her arm out of my grip and lunged for him.

'Whoa, darling. Careful with the goods.' He said as he slipped around one of his friends, narrowly evading her. Patience pushed the boy he was hiding behind hard on his shoulders causing him to topple over the idiot crouching behind him. I leaned into my microphone to speak with dispatch about sending anyone else in Chatham to our location. Just in case.

'Come here, tiny penis.' Patience growled as she grabbed him by the collar with both hands. She hefted him clean off the ground and bounced him off a handy shop window. The general crowd of shoppers passing by didn't even bother to look – young men getting slapped about by the police was a daily occurrence in Chatham.

'Hey, babe no need to get frisky. I don't want to see your boobs, just the pretty white girl's.' He was still laughing and joking, not realising he had just kicked a bear.

'What? You disrespectful little turd. You don't want to see my tits? You couldn't handle my tits. My tits would break your tiny little dick in two.'

Then she kneed him in the nuts, but she achieved this by sweeping his feet out on either side and leaving her knee sticking out for him to fall on. Now far less resistant, Patience dragged him around the corner out of sight. Several of his friends looked ready to bolt as I tried to corral them around the corner as well. They might have done so had two more uniforms not been running towards us through the crowd.

They were armed police, there were two on permanent rotation in Chatham, often hanging out in the Pentagon shopping mall as that was where the most people were. Patience and I had spotted them in the distance on our way in.

'Help you, ladies?' The taller of the two asked slightly out of breath. 'Dispatch said officer in need of assistance. Made it sound urgent.' The two men would be from the Chatham station, so they were vaguely familiar, but I didn't know them. Chances were though that they knew Patience as she had transferred to Maidstone from Chatham some years ago and was not the sort of person one forgot. Ever.

'Ooh!' said the chap next to him as Patience cuffed the young man and in so doing accidentally, very much on purpose, knelt on his testicles. The poor boy let out a yelp. His now sheepish friends were looking at each other, looking at the ground. One took out his phone and held it up as if to start filming the event.

'I would put that away unless you want it inserted somewhere.' The taller guy whispered to him. He turned to me. 'I once heard that she caught two guys chasing a girl and she gaffer-taped them together with their pants around their ankles and top to tail, so each had to look at the other's todger.

I raised my eyebrows but could not honestly say that the story surprised me.

Patience appeared to be done with the young man. She lifted him up using the cuffs, which is something we are not allowed to do and wheeled him around to face his friends. 'Now, what it is that you have to say to the assembled gentlemen?' she prompted him.

The boy had tears on his face and looked quite sick. He also had dirt all over the front of his clothing where Patience had him on the ground. It was the usual expensive but crap sportswear that all his friends were also modelling a derivative of. He did not seem inclined to speak. Patience did something behind his back, most likely giving the cuffs a twist and he started talking right away.

'I am very sorry for my lewd comments. Err, I have no right to objectify women of any age and most especially ladies in positions of responsibility such as police officers.'

'And?'

'And I want all my friends to learn from my poor example and the consequences I have suffered for my ill-thought choices.'

'And?'

The boy turned his head miserably to look at her. He didn't want to say anything more.

'And?' she prompted again, a little venom in her tone.

He hung his head, unable to look at anyone. 'And I have a tiny penis.' His friends burst into laughter until Patience shot them a wide-eyed look of warning.

'Very good, Antony. See how easy that was.' Patience fiddled behind his back and the cuffs came off. Now you and your friends can go play but remember to be nice to ladies and be gentlemanly at all times.

I picked up the box of cameras.

'That was fun.' The taller guy said. 'You two should come down here more often.'

'Feeling better?' I asked Patience as she brushed dirt from her palms.

'Much better, thank you. Shall we get this done then?'

We arrived at the first bank of lifts and pressed the call button to bring it to us. The door pinged immediately and opened. The lifts were not sophisticated enough to have a screen that showed what floor it was on. I got in and turned to press the button. We were on the ground floor so the only way to go was up. I noticed that Patience was not with me. Nor was she stood in front of the open doors.

I stuck my head back outside, holding the door open with one hand. 'Patience, what are you doing?' she was skulking just a few feet away, looking guilty.

'I will wait here for you. You don't need me in the lift, do you?'

I stared at her. 'Are you afraid of the ghost?'

'I can feel its evil presence from here, Amanda. You wanna be a Ghostbuster now, that's your business. Patience ain't getting in no ghost lift.' Her eyes were bugging out a bit and she was shaking her head.

'You have got to be kidding me. Look, I need your help, I cannot fit the cameras by myself, so you're going to have to put your brave girl pants on and ride the lift with me for ten seconds.'

'Uh-uh.' she replied backing away.

I put the box down to trap the door and went to grab her. 'Get in the damned lift.' She danced away, but I snagged her protective vest and pulled her off balance. We were tucked down a short corridor, so not visible to the people walking through the shopping centre but several people had now stopped at the mouth of the corridor having seen movement and were watching us tussle.

I finally pushed her into the lift, the first of eight that I needed to go in and the lift doors shut. Patience was backed against the far wall now, eyes darting in every direction.

'It's cold in here, Amanda. Why is it so cold?'

I opened my mouth to assure her that it was the same temperature as everywhere else, but she cut me off.

'Because the ghost is coming to get us, that's why.' Her legs appeared barely able to support her bodyweight. She was slumped into the corner holding herself up with a hand against two walls.

Ignoring her, I took the first camera from the box and discovering that the ceiling was lower than I thought, I fitted it in place. It had a magnetic attachment. I turned it on and quickly checked the feed to the laptop Tempest had given me. This was the lift that had scored the most incidents, the one next to it the second highest number. I fitted an infrared camera next to the first one. Doubling up the cameras like this meant I could only cover six lifts but I was gambling that these would be the ones that would score me a result. Now I would get an image whether the lights were on or off.

The lift pinged, and the doors opened. Patience burst into action, bolting for the exit. She hit the doors before they were even halfway open, her equipment clanging against both sides as she forced her way through the gap. Sighing, I picked up the box and followed her out.

'I need to fit cameras in another five lifts, Patience.' Patience was ten feet away across the car park that the lift had opened on.

She waggled a finger at me. 'I am not going back in any stupid lifts. I can't believe you made me do that.'

'Patience it is just a lift. A big steel box.'

'Yeah. With a ghost in it. You go ahead and do what you got to do, girl. I am going back to the car. Matter of fact, I am taking my lunch break. Patience needs a sandwich.' And with that, she stomped off towards the stairwell.

A lot of help she turned out to be. It was a good thing I had overestimated the height of the ceiling in the lifts. I could reach it easily on my toes.

Twenty minutes later, I had the last of the cameras in place and had only once had to quickly stop what I was doing because someone was trying to get on. I found Patience happily sitting in the same booth as yesterday tucking into another party platter. Her hands were greasy all the way to her wrists, but she looked content.

'Hey there, partner. How are you doing now?' I asked sliding into the booth opposite her.

'Mmmm.' she said through a mouthful of bread. 'Much better. Sorry about before. I kinda freaked out a bit. Do you really think there is no ghost?'

'Yes, Patience. I have no doubt whatsoever that it is not a ghost stealing people's shopping. I'll tell you what. When I work out who is behind this, I will get you to perform the arrest. Ok?'

I had her attention now. 'Really? You would do that? Just turn them over for me to have the collar?'

'Sure. I don't need it. It will not help my career in the Police with only a couple of weeks left. Besides, I will be performing this investigation as the employee of a private investigation firm and as such my remit is to determine the solution to the case, not to make the arrest. In a couple of weeks, my powers of arrest are gone along with my Police ID, so I might as well get used to it.' This was something Tempest had gone over a few times. Clients needed to understand that we found out what was going on, we presented an explanation for their mystery but if there was a criminal perpetrating the odd goings on then we handed it over to the police. Every time.

'Well, you could have said that before. I could have helped with the cameras if you had said that.' Patience was rooting around in the bottom of the bucket, scooping out the last few fries. Quite how she put it all away without bursting out of her uniform I had no idea. She carried a few extra pounds but no more than that, yet she ate like a bear preparing for hibernation.

The radios squawked again. There was a traffic accident they wanted us to attend. Dispatch wanted to know our ETA. The accident was at the top of Bluebell Hill – somewhere that accidents occurred all too regularly, and we were at least fifteen minutes away. I lied and told them five.

Patience and I locked eyes for a second, then jumped out of our seats to run back to the car.

'Dammit! My hat!' Patience yelled as we got outside. She had left it in the booth. I left her to fetch it while I went to get the car.

In My Flat. Wednesday, October 20th 1917hrs

The RTA had taken up the rest of the shift. It had been a proper pile-up. Five cars had been mashed into one enormous mess with a further six cars suffering damage as they tried to avoid the carnage in front of them. At the top of the Bluebell Hill, the road leading from the motorway merged onto the dual carriageway leading from Chatham to Maidstone. Traffic on the dual carriageway was always fast moving and to compensate, the cars trying to merge did so at speed. Sometimes someone gets it wrong and auto-violence ensues.

Despite that, our shift had ended more or less on time and I had taken myself home looking forward to three days off. I stopped on the way back to my flat to buy wine and a pizza, dropped the pizza by the oven as I walked through the house and had the top off the wine and the bottle to my lips before I got to the bathroom to turn on the bath.

Soaking in the bath with a book and a goblet of wine, I remembered the cameras. I had forgotten about them with the trauma and drama of the afternoon.

The laptop and the box the cameras came in was still in the boot of my car. It would have to wait, but I was curious to see if I had captured anything. As it turned out I had.

Half an hour later I was finishing off my glass of wine, which was now getting warm and I was sitting on my small sofa, in my small flat with the laptop perched on my lap. On the sofa next to me were the remains of the pizza which consisted of four crusts and a few crumbs. I called up the camera feed and set the time back to when I had put them in earlier today. I had the feed from all eight cameras going at once and the speed set to ten times normal. Mostly I was looking at empty lifts, but with the clock whizzing along, a blur would occur periodically as someone, or several someones, got on and then got off again. I could not tell, of course, if the lifts were going up or down, only that people were getting on and off. The two infrared cameras showed a glassy white image in which I could detect vague movement but nothing else.

I stared at the screen for fifteen minutes. It was getting boring. I did some mental calculation. I had roughly six hours of footage, but the shops had shut at six o'clock so probably only four hours were worth looking at. Therefore, I should only have about twenty-four minutes of footage to scan at high speed.

Was that right?

I did the maths again and decided I was correct. Then one of the screens went black, it was just a blip that had lasted perhaps one second but watching it in fast forward meant at least ten seconds had passed. I clicked pause and ran the footage back. Then played it at normal speed. In the lift was a middle-aged lady. She was standing still in the middle of the lift, both hands by her sides with heavy shopping in them. Then she put the bags in her left hand down and began fishing in her handbag. Probably looking for her car keys.

The lights went out and it was pitch black. I could see nothing on the screen at all. It was not one of the lifts I had fitted an infrared camera in, so I continued to watch until the lights came back on. The lady was now flat against the wall to her right, her mouth open like she had been screaming. As I watched, her head turned to the right and she darted out of picture clearly exiting the lift. I rewound it and played it again. Then again and then again.

I mapped out the event on an A4 pad.

- Victim puts down her bag
- One second later the lights go out

- Twenty-two seconds later the lights come back on
- Four seconds after that she runs out of the screen when presumably the lift doors open
- The bag she put on the floor is not in either of her hands and is not visibly in the lift either

I watched it one more time but decided I could learn very little from it. I elected to email Martin Miller though and ask if the lady had reported the incident. I would interview her if she had.

I went back to watching the footage at ten times speed. The number of people getting in and out of the lifts increased for a period. I reasoned that it was probably close to closing time, so I was witnessing the rush to leave. As the numbers tailed off and I was about to give up, another lift went black. I pressed pause and my heart skipped – it was one of the lifts with an infrared camera fitted. What had been a glassy white blur was now a weird other-worldly image, but it was sharp and clear. With the screen paused I could see the two people in the lift, a young couple in their thirties were caught midway through their shocked reaction.

I took the footage back again as I had before and watched it at normal speed. The couple got in as a mother and her two small children got out. They were talking, their faces relaxed, so not arguing but having a conversation as a couple might. The chap had bags in each hand, his petite girlfriend was carrying nothing although I could see when he turned, that the bags were all from ladies' fashion shops. He put the bags in his right hand down and shot his cuff to check his watch. Then the lights went out.

I moved my gaze down to stare at the infrared screen. The girlfriend was clearly screaming and had clung to the man who was also looking panicked. Then, as I watched, a panel in the wall of the lift opened and a figure climbed out. All the hair on the back of my neck stood on end. It was wearing dark clothing and had on a balaclava and gloves. It leaned out, took a short pace, snagged the shopping bags from the floor and retreated inside the panel. Two seconds later the lights came back on. The figure was distinctly male.

I rewound it and watched again, this time at half speed. The cameras were not sophisticated enough to allow me to zoom in – they were designed to be small and unobtrusive over other features plus I was watching it recorded not live. The man in the mask could be anyone at this point, but I had a good idea who it was already. I smiled a smile like the Grinch at Christmas, plotting my cunning plan and looking forward to solving the case. It had been easier than I had expected, but I had not caught anyone yet.

I closed the laptop, drained my wine glass and wondered if I could have another and not have a buzzing head in the morning. The clock on my wall was saying that it was only half past eight, so I picked up the remote and found some trashy TV to watch.

I would catch my first ghost tomorrow.

Ghostbusting. Thursday, October 21st 0745hrs

I awoke with a dryness to my mouth that I put down to the wine I had guiltily finished last night. While I was slouched on the sofa with my feet curled under me, I had found a favourite movie from years ago that had just started and had stayed up later than I had intended. The lateness led to another glass of wine, the wine led to a bag of M&Ms, so now I was lying in bed wondering if the calories last night needed to be worked off this morning. I knew that they did, of course. I was just trying to find the effort to do something about it. The clock by my bed told me it was quarter to eight. What I really wanted to do was roll over, go back to sleep and wake up to find that I had only dreamt of drinking a whole bottle of wine and eating chocolate.

Ten minutes later I had on skin tight stretchy pants and running shoes, my best sports bra, a light top, plus a pair of thin gloves. I put the key under the doormat, stretched in place for a moment and reluctantly set off. My usual running route was almost five miles and took me around forty minutes. I did not embrace running. However, I accepted that it was a necessary part of my life even though I was not a fan.

It was cold out, not as bad as yesterday and it was dry – I would not have gone if it was raining. I got into a pace I was happy with as I headed down towards the river. My hair, which I had pulled into a ponytail, swished from side to side behind my head, keeping time with my feet. I crossed the road by Maidstone football ground, passed the rowing club and emerged onto the riverside path where yesterday's rain was still visible.

Dodging puddles, mud, and piles of mess left by irresponsible dog-owners, I began to push myself. I passed the spot where I had met Tempest, just past the place where Victoria Turnbull had been murdered by *The Vampire* a few weeks ago. In my head, I could still see the crime scene tape. Then I passed the River Angel public house and the path alongside the river terminated as it reached a weir. I crossed over the river using the path over the top of the weir and began the hard climb up the hill on the other side.

I clicked my stopwatch off at thirty-eight minutes and twelve seconds just as I reached my building. Not bad. I had been thinking about the day ahead as I had run. I really wanted to catch the ghost today and close the case. It would be nice to feel that I was earning the money Tempest had already started paying me. He had insisted he pay me a full wage in typical Tempest style. To me, it had seemed that he ought to pay me for the hours I was working but he expressed that since I was committed enough to work both jobs simultaneously, the least he could do was make it worth my effort. Although the focus of my thoughts was on the case, I also had a date tonight to consider. Brett was taking me out for food. This was date two if one was content to consider the weekend in Paris as one date, which meant that the next time I saw him after this would be date three and that had potential implications.

I had not had a relationship that was worth labelling as such for over a year now. The last properly serious one was more than two years ago. The problem always seemed to be that boys were such utter twats. I had always been cheated on or messed about. Childhood dreams of whirlwind romances, fancy weddings and happy family picnics in the park had given inevitable way to a focus on my career because it was something I could rely upon. Now though, there was a tiny spark of hope inside me that Brett might be the real thing. I reminded my hopeful inner self continually that he and I had only been on one date and had not slept together yet.

With towels wrapped around my hair and my body to keep in the warmth of the shower, I studied my wardrobe and ignored the voice inside screaming that I had nothing to wear. I had no money to buy a new outfit either, so I was going to have to make do. My favourite jeans were in the laundry basket. Could I wash then dry them and have them ready to wear tonight? They went so well with my blue satin halter-neck top and the pairing worked with my good coat and bag. I was going out for dinner with a millionaire – I needed to look good. Oh, but what about the knitted dress I bought with my birthday money? It was by Hobbs and looked brand new still as I had only worn it once so far. The deliberation went on for a while.

Finally dressed for the day and my outfit (probably) picked out for tonight I settled back in front of the laptop and watched the elevator footage yet again. My excitement last night had been a little premature. I could see how the crime was being perpetrated but I had no useable evidence regarding the criminal's identity. I had a plan. My only question was whether it would work or not. I was likely to have more success if I had help, but I was being stubborn and intended to produce the answer to the mystery and the person behind it all by myself.

Yeah. Strike one up for woman!

It was time to get on with it. I grabbed a few items I believed I would need, went out to my car and drove to Chatham. On the way I phoned Patience.

'Hey, girl.' she answered. 'What'cha doing?'

'I am back at the Pentagon. I am catching the ghost today.' I went on to outline what I had seen on the laptop last night and what I planned to do today. I then asked her to look something up for me. My theory had an unknown element to it, which was all to do with what happened to the goods in the shopping bags after they had been stolen.

Patience was back on the dispatch desk today and might struggle to get away, but she was going to find time to get me the information I needed and if necessary, coordinate the response that might follow.

I checked my watch. It was almost quarter past ten.

Time to go to work.

I needed to check the charge on the cameras. The battery life was about twenty-four hours, so they would all be about to run out if they had not already. They had all been working when I checked them this morning on the laptop, but they had been recording all night since there was no way to remotely switch them off. I couldn't do much about them running out, but I had brought the charging units with me. I planned to retrieve them all and get Martin to charge them up again in his office.

I arrived at the Pentagon shopping mall and paid for a full day's parking. I could charge it to expenses, Tempest assured me this was necessary as such things were tax deductible. I pushed open the doors that led from the carpark to the shops and emerged by Superdrug on the ground floor.

The shopping centre was quiet again this morning. I could not tell whether it was more quiet than usual or not but there were very few people around.

Collecting all the cameras took almost an hour. I had to ride the same lift up and down on more than one occasion as there were people in the lift with me. The task done though, I called Martin Miller. It took him a while to answer and when he finally came on the phone, he sounded sleepy and distant.

'Hello?'

'Mr. Miller? This is Amanda Harper from the Blue Moon Investigation Agency.'

'Oh. Good morning. How may I help you?' he asked, audibly stifling a yawn.

'I have a lead on your ghost. I believe I may solve the case soon.' The term soon quite deliberately not being a measurable unit of time. 'I need to charge some equipment in your office.'

'Oh. Sorry. I am not at work today. It was my birthday yesterday, I was out late and took today off. I have a bit of a hangover.' It was more information than I needed. The pertinent fact was that he was not at work and I would have to manage without the cameras for now.

I thanked him and said that I had to go.

'Hold on.' he pleaded. 'You said you think you know what is going on. What is it?'

I stayed quiet for a second deciding what I wanted to tell him. 'I will be able to give you a full report later, Martin. For now, it would be wrong of me to speculate. I can tell you that you do not have a ghost, just a clever criminal.' I disconnected and put my phone away.

Back at my car, I swapped the box of cameras for the bags I had in the boot. I was going to pose as a shopper. What I had seen on the footage last night made me believe that the ghost was hiding in a false panel that had been built into the lifts during the recent refit. I had looked for and immediately found a small spy hole in the panel. From it, the ghost was able to watch the people inside the lift. If they had shopping and put it down, the ghost would flip a switch to kill the power, step out, snag the bags and get back inside the panel. That was my theory anyway.

What I had not been able to establish, was how the panel was accessed. I had inspected every lift that I had gone into this morning. All six of them were the same design and same dimensions and since ghost attacks had been reported from each it seemed logical that each of them contained the same hidden compartment.

I had six shopping bags, three for each hand. I had dug them out of the little bag receptacle in my kitchen where I stuffed bags in case they came in handy for something. These had been in there for months and they were badly crumpled which had necessitated some clever use of a pillowcase and my iron to make them look flat and new again. They didn't really look new and would not fool anyone if they took a close look, but I gauged that a man peering through a tiny spy-hole would not be able to tell the difference. From my closet, I had filled them with some folded clothes and an old shoe box I had kept.

I picked the lift that I had seen the ghost in yesterday, got in and rode it up from the ground floor to the sixth floor at the top of the car park. Then I rode it down again. Nothing happened. I realised my mistake and got out. I got into the lift next to it, its pair in the bank of lifts and pressed the button to go up again. This time I put my bags down, encouraging the ghost to flip the switch and grab them.

The lift pinged to announce my arrival at the top floor again. I pursed my lips. No ghost. I rode the lift back down again, arrived on the ground floor, picked up my bags and picked a different bank of lifts to try. I got the same result there and at the next bank of lifts and at all the others. Somewhat deflated, I went for coffee.

Stupid, unreliable ghost.

With a tall flat white in my hand, I slumped into a chair in the open-air coffee shop and wondered what to try next. Do I just keep going with the

72

same tactic? If I want to try something different, what would that be? My phone pinged with a text. I took a sip of coffee and swiped my phone screen to open it.

I had two text messages. The first from Tempest wishing me good luck today, the second from Patience, telling me that I was right, and that she had found it. Her message went on to ask what I wanted her to do next. I had been playing a hunch when I had asked her to perform a quick task this morning. It had probably only taken her a few minutes once she had a break from work but was key to unravelling the mystery. I sent her a reply asking her to wait and promising to get back to her later.

I gave myself a mental shake. I was going to catch the ghost today. I just needed to be patient and keep going. I would target all the lifts, moving between the banks until I got lucky. The attacks did not happen every day, but I could not let the possibility that the ghost had taken the day off deter me.

My watch told me it was just a few minutes after twelve o'clock. I finished my coffee and went back to riding the lifts. I can report that riding lifts is boring. By two o'clock my feet were sore, making me wish I had worn my running shoes, my back was aching, and I had had quite enough of staring at the inside of a lift. My stomach growled its insistence that I put something in it, so I trudged back to the coffee shop where I ordered another coffee and a roasted vegetable panini.

I allowed myself a thirty-minute lunch break but ten minutes in I got the latest update from Steve Brooms. There had been an incident in the right-hand lift of the orange lift bank.

Dammit! I had just been in that lift.

I left the last few bites of my panini, as it wasn't all that nice and headed for the lifts. A small circle was visible close to where I wanted to go. Sure enough, in the centre of it was a young woman in tears along with security guard Karl, who waved a hello as he spotted me and a chap in a suit who I was fairly sure would prove to be Steve Brooms. I had yet to meet him, but he fit my mental picture having listened to his voice and he appeared to be taking charge of the situation. He had a radio in his left hand and had his name on a badge pinned to the right lapel of his cheap suit. Beneath the name, it said Head of Security. I quickly introduced myself and quietly insisted that we take the lady to one of the backroom offices so that we could take her statement.

Steve had looked like he was going to argue but instead, he nodded and led her away. I wondered if the girl was upset because it had been another sexual attack. Had the ghost grabbed her as he had Poppy? I then wondered how many other girls might have been fondled but not reported it. Experience told me that for every victim that came forward there were many more that did not.

That was not the case though she assured me. She was upset because she had just bought herself a bracelet in Pandora and some new underwear and a pair of shoes. Her boyfriend was a soldier at the local Army unit, but he was in Afghanistan currently, so had sent her money for her birthday with instructions on what to get herself. There was a lot of sobbing in her retelling of the incident.

I had missed the ghost by a minute or so. Had I ridden the lift again it might have been me. I was annoyed and could not decide if I was more annoyed that the ghost had not picked me to attack or that I now had to go back to riding the lifts once more. The ghost was here today. I had to hope he would strike again.

I left Steve and Karl to deal with the tearful young woman and went back to the lifts. Did I try the orange lifts again or would he have moved on to a different one? I figured it was absolute guesswork, so I went to the nearest bank of lifts and pressed the call button to summon one of them. Seconds later the right-hand lift pinged, and the doors swished open. I stepped in and got an instant hit of garlic sausage. I suddenly knew that this was the smell that people had been trying to describe to me. I also knew that I was breathing in the smell of Charles Spencer's farts.

Wrinkling my nose and putting up with it, I turned around to face back towards the doors and put my shopping down. I pressed the button for the top floor. Just as the doors closed a hand snuck through the gap and stopped them. Two boys in their late teens got in as the doors reopened. They were laughing about something and barely acknowledged my presence. The taller of the two leaned across and pressed the button for floor five.

My heart was beating hard when the doors finally closed, and the lift started moving. I was convinced that this was it. Any second now...

Then the lift pinged and stopped at the second floor to let on an old couple. The two boys moved further back into the corner of the lift. It was getting crowded in the small steel box and it would have been more polite for me to pick my bags up and move, but I kept myself and my shopping next to the panel. I needed to be ready. The doors shut just as the old man pressed the button for floor four. I had only a few seconds now until the lift would stop again. Would the ghost attack now?

The lights went out and the lift jolted to a halt.

One of the boys let out a squeak.

'Danny, you faggot.' His friend laughed.

Then I felt it. There was movement next to me. I could not see anything but that didn't stop me from acting. Imagining where the ghost might be, I turned towards it and reached out with both hands. I intended to grab hold, get the person into a lock and subdue them. At that second, I realised that once I had done so I would still be trapped in a lift with no power or light and could not get out, but too late now, I was committed.

My right hand caught hold of an arm, which shoved me away. I lost my balance momentarily but threw myself back at the place it had been, grasping for purchase again. This time I got a good hold. The ghost had his hands full of my shopping bags, which he tried once again to use to push me away. He was retreating into the hidden compartment. I pushed off my left foot, stepped into him and kicked my right knee upwards. Hard.

It connected. There was an audible outrushing of breath and the figure I was holding doubled over.

I followed him down to the floor of the elevator and knelt on his back. 'Oh, my balls!' he groaned pathetically. I needed light to be sure, but the voice sounded like it was Charlie. He had curled into a foetal position. I had hit his nuts hard – he was going nowhere.

Suddenly the interior of the lift was bathed in light. One of the guys had turned on the light on his phone. The other chap did likewise, making it almost as bright as it had been with the main light on.

Beneath me was a man wearing a mask.

'What the devil is going on?' asked the old man. He was backed into a corner with his wife pushed behind him protectively.

'All is well, Sir. This man is a thief that has been plaguing the Pentagon and stealing shopping using a false panel he fitted in the lifts.' I explained without taking my eyes off the man beneath me. He was groaning softly now and nursing his testicles with both hands.

'I told you we should have gone to Bluewater.' The old man's wife complained, referring to the bigger and newer shopping mall a few miles away.

'Guys.' I said looking over my shoulder at the two younger men. 'Can one of you please check inside the panel and see if you can find a switch to turn the power back on?'

'Err, yeah.' One said. He had to climb over me to get to the panel and peer inside it, but he found the switch almost straight away. The light flicked back on and the lift started moving.

I pulled out my phone and called Steve Brooms. 'Steve?' I confirmed when he answered. 'I have your ghost. Meet me on the ground floor of the blue lift bank in two minutes. Okay?'

He said that he would. He sounded shocked.

The lift pinged as we reached the fourth floor and the old couple got off looking thankful to be able to leave. Still kneeling on the ghost's back, I turned to the two young men again and asked them if they would kindly accompany me back to the ground floor where I would be met by security. They said they were happy to do it. The lift continued to the fifth floor and to the sixth because it knew no better than to do as it had originally been instructed, then started back down again. It stopped on the third floor where a family of five wanted to get on. With shocked faces, they elected to wait for the next one.

Charlie appeared to be recovering from his abdominal discomfort. He was beginning to move about and make noises.

'Get off me.' he demanded. I ignored him. The lift was on its way down now, just passing floor two. 'Get off me.' he repeated with more force and volume.

I grabbed his stupid mask and ripped it off. It was Charlie beneath the mask, and as habit would have it, he farted. I felt it vibrate through my whole body and since I was kneeling on his back the stench of it hit me as I took my very next breath.

I gagged. It was disgusting. The lift pinged, and the doors opened. Steve Brooms, Karl the security guard and three other chaps in the same security guard uniform were outside. They were blocking my exit, but I was leaving anyway before I threw up. I rolled off Charlie and into the fresher air outside, coming to rest at Steve's feet. The two young men were trying to get out as well and the security detachment was trying to get in. The doorway became a jam of bodies. Charlie saw his opportunity and dived back through the false panel. It shut behind him just as security guard Karl's fingers grabbed for it. Through their legs, I could see that he had escaped.

I had been beaten by a fart!

'Quick, guys. We need to get to the back of the lift shaft. He is getting in and out through the maintenance hatches.' I was grabbing Steve's arm while I said this and dragging him back to where I knew we could access the maintenance areas. Then we were running, the security guards coming along behind us. I glanced back to see the pudgy face of security guard Karl falling behind.

Steve fumbled for his pass as we reached the door, buzzed it open and lead the way through and down to the lift shaft that I had been shown by Charlie and Jack a couple of days ago.

He was gone when we got there.

Dammit.

I checked the time and pulled out my phone. It connected, and a voice came on the other end.

'Hey, girl...'

I interrupted her rudely. 'Patience, where are you? Are you still in uniform?' It was two minutes past three, so she should have just finished her shift. If she wanted this collar it was now or never. I explained what I needed her to do and where she needed to go, then I told Steve to find Jack and to hold him and ran back to my car.

This morning I had tasked Patience with finding where Jack and Charlie lived and with looking for the list of stolen goods on eBay. They might be selling them anywhere but new in box items were easy to shift on eBay, so it was my best guess. She had tasked her sister and mother with looking for a seller that was selling multiple items new in box from the list of stolen shopping. Since the shopping had been taken from people of all ages and genders it was a very odd mix to be selling and ought to stand out instantly. I had been right as it had taken them less than an hour to find a seller with almost all the stolen goods listed. Patience had then been able to obtain the name and address of the seller using my PayPal account to purchase an item for collection. I had no idea what she had bought but since it was stolen goods it would be going back to the owner anyway.

The address was Charlie's. At this stage, I could not tell if Jack was also involved but it seemed likely. Highly likely given that they both maintained the lifts and refitting them with the hidden compartment could not have been a one-man job.

Charlie lived at an address in Walderslade. It was halfway between where I was in Chatham and where Patience was in Maidstone and about ten minutes' drive for either of us provided the traffic played along. I was impatient and got stuck behind an immaculate 1982 Vauxhall Chevette. It was being driven by what appeared to be a dead body going at snail's pace up the Maidstone road. There was nowhere to pass, so I pootled along, swearing under my breath until he finally turned off.

I shot forward as there was no traffic ahead of me, took the corner at Pattens Lane on what felt like two wheels and headed down Waterworks Hill at a speed that bordered on dangerous. I suddenly had flashing lights in my rear-view mirror.

I swore again, but I had only a few hundred yards left to go, so I kept going, certain they would follow me. I turned off the main road, took a side street and screeched to a halt in front of the address I had for him. Patience had pulled up seconds ahead of me and was just getting out of her car.

The squad car chasing me also screeched to halt, its sirens blaring.

'What the hell, Amanda?' demanded Brad Hardacre as he bailed out of his car and recognised me.

'Hi, Brad. Arrest to make. Thanks for the assist.' He had been planning nothing of the sort when he gave chase, but he conceded and came with us anyway. Both he and Mike Bayfoot, the fellow driving the car, got out and came with Patience and me.

The arrest was an anti-climax though. The front door opened as we went up the driveway to Charlie's house. Charlie was standing in the doorway looking glum. He had nowhere to go and as we found out when we got inside, he had altogether far too may stolen items to hide. Patience read him his rights and slapped the cuffs on. Brad and Mike took him away just as other officers arrived to begin the process of cataloguing the stolen goods.

Stood amid the bags and boxes spread out in his living room, dining room and kitchen, it was apparent that he had stolen far, far more than had been reported. I breathed in deeply and let myself relax. I felt good. I had caught the damned ghost and it had only taken me a couple of days while I was simultaneously holding down another full-time job. I had been so nervous about quitting my steady, but boring job in the Police. It was stable, and I was swapping it for an undefined role in a new business where the firm investigated people's paranormal mysteries. I felt rewarded though for the first time in so long that I could not even remember getting the same feeling at any time in the Police.

'Here you go.' Patience said handing me an Ann Summers bag.

'What's this?' I asked her.

'It is what you bought on eBay.' She was grinning at me. I didn't like that she was grinning. I looked in the bag. There was an utterly insubstantial pair of knickers and matching bra. They were so pointless they could have been spun from spider's web. I hooked them out with one finger and held them up. 'That's not all.' Patience said, still grinning.

I noticed that the bag was too heavy to be empty. I peered inside once more. At the bottom of the bag was a giant vibrator.

FFS.

'What is wrong with you, Patience? Why on earth would you buy me a vibrator?'

'Hey, I didn't buy it, girl. It was your PayPal account. Seems to me you need some encouragement with your sex life anyhow. There you are surrounded by fine men and you ain't sleeping with any of them. Big Ben, Tempest, Brett.' she said counting them off on her fingers. 'I don't know why you ever have your knickers on.'

I rolled my eyes and put the bag down. It was stolen goods, so it would be catalogued along with everything else and go back to its rightful owner, assuming they could find her.

My part in this case was concluded. I had already made a call to Martin Miller and explained who his ghost was. He had already heard it from Steve Brooms, his head of security but I gave him the more complete story and of course the detail of what had happened after I left the Pentagon. Astonishingly, Martin sounded quite dejected by my news. Losing both of his lift service engineers meant he was not allowed to have the lifts in operation it seemed and that presented him with a bigger problem than he had with the ghost. Jack and Charlie were of course in it together. Jack had confessed as soon as Steve had confronted him. They had hatched the plan over a year ago when the lift refit was proposed. Incredibly it was not even their idea. They were copying something they had read about in an industry magazine after a similar case had occurred in South Korea a while ago. They would go to jail, I was certain of that, but the firm could bill the hours and report another successful case and that was what was important to me now.

The next call was to Tempest. He answered almost before the phone started ringing.

'Amanda. How goes it?'

'The ghost case is concluded. I am just wrapping things up now. It was the lift engineers behind it.' He listened while I explained what they had been doing and how they had been doing it. I needed to file a report that would go to the client with the invoice and submit my expenses as they were catalogued by the case where possible. Jane would handle all the paperwork, I just needed to fill it out.

'Amanda, I would love to be able to say that I am duly impressed, but I never had any doubt that you would be a natural at this. Despite that, I must congratulate you on the successful conclusion of your first case. Well done.' He managed to not sound patronising, it was great to hear his praise. I am a big girl and shouldn't need my ego massaged but I welcomed his comments nevertheless.

I was free the next day, so I agreed to see him at the office at 0900hrs (he insisted on using a twenty-four-hour clock whenever he made time references) where we would look at new cases.

Patience was waiting outside by her car for me to leave the house. In a rare moment of seriousness, she thanked me for giving her the collar. We hugged and went to our separate cars. It felt like it had been a long day. I was hungry, but then I had eaten half a panini since breakfast and it was now quarter past six in the evening.

I had a date tonight and needed to get home for a bath and spruce up. Could my hunger wait until I was out tonight? I didn't think so, but I had fruit in the house and that would keep me going without ruining my appetite.

On the short drive home, I thought about what Patience had said about my sex life. Was I too concerned about being labelled? Should I just get some every now and then like she did? I was not sure how well that would sit with me, but my thoughts turned to Brett and whether the same rules applied to him. After a date tonight and the weekend in Paris, the idea of feeling his weight on top of me was appealing. Was he just waiting for me to decide the waiting period was over and then prove that I was worth the wait? How long would he wait for that matter? He was firmly placed in the eligible male category and like Patience had said he could probably have any woman he wanted including models, actresses, and famous heiresses. What was it that I was waiting for?

I told myself to shut up and enjoy my evening out. Brett would be along soon, there would be another case tomorrow and I felt like I had nothing to worry about. Was I going to end up marrying Brett? Unlikely. I had been on one date with him. He was good-looking, and he was rich, but I really didn't know anything about what he was like as a person. Maybe he would have a tiny penis. I distinctly doubted it, yet I could not rule out the possibility that, notwithstanding all the boxes he was already ticking, there might be a deal breaker in there somewhere.

I parked my car with that thought reverberating around my head. Now I needed to find out.

A Date with Brett. Thursday, October 21st 1911hrs

I gave serious consideration to buying a bottle of champagne on my way home. I felt like I ought to be celebrating my success with a liquid high five. I resisted though, knowing that not only could I not afford to buy myself a decent brand, but I would also then be stuck with an entire bottle to drink by myself. Plus, I was going out with Brett tonight so really ought to be sober when he turned up to collect me. I wondered then what car he would be driving. I was quite certain he had several to choose from, so would we be in a chauffeur-driven Roller? A Lamborghini? The Batmobile? I would find out soon enough.

Stood in my bedroom, having finally dressed in what I was adamantly telling myself was the final outfit choice for the night, I turned and checked how I looked in the mirror. On the bed behind me were more than half the outfits I owned. Each had been held up, tried on, rejected and now required hanging or folding and putting away. I still wasn't one hundred percent happy with what I was wearing.

Just then the doorbell rang. I glanced at the clock by my bed. It was too early for Brett. At least I thought it was, but perhaps he was just really keen. I moved to the window and glanced out. I could not see a flash looking car in the street.

The doorbell rang again before I could get to it. It wasn't Brett outside though, it was Tempest, holding a large bunch of flowers and a bottle of Dom Perignon.

'Good evening, Amanda. I hope I am not disturbing you.'

'Not at all, Tempest. These are lovely.' I said, taking the flowers from him. It was a large spray of stargazer lilies, a few of which were already open, their fragrant smell instantly recognisable. 'Come in, please.'

I took the flowers to the kitchen to find a vase to place them in. I was certain I owned one. Tempest shut the door as he came through it.

'Are you sure I am not interrupting your evening?'

'Not at all.' I replied.

'Okay. When I solved my first case it was just me at the business and I had no one to celebrate with. It felt appropriate to acknowledge your success.'

'You are very generous, Tempest.' He had followed me into my flat and was standing holding the champagne in a way that suggested he was waiting for me to take it. I placed the flowers in the sink, popped the plug in the hole and ran some water. I would deal with them later when I had found the damned vase's hiding place. I took the bottle from him. It was cold and ready to be savoured.

I glanced at the clock. I still had a while before Brett was due. 'Would you like a glass with me? Toast our future success?'

'Are you not going out?' I guess it was clear from my outfit that I was not dressed for a night on the sofa watching soap operas.

I smiled and started fiddling with the cork. I might let Brett come in for a glass and some snogging after dinner with the excuse that I had an open bottle of champagne going flat. I doubted I would need an excuse though.

'Do you have time?' I asked Tempest, just before I levered the cork out.

'Sure. I'm not going anywhere for a while.' With a pop and a gentle fizz, the cork came free. It pinged off the ceiling and hit the end of a spoon next to the sink where last night's discarded bowl of soup was sitting. The spoon jumped and sprayed Tempest with icky red tomato-based gloop.

It seemed to happen in slow-motion with the pair of us watching the red liquid flying through the air. Some of it hit his face, but the majority of it landed on his expensive-looking white shirt.

Typical.

'Oh.' He said. 'Do you, ah... Do you mind if I get some water on this?' His fingers were already on his buttons, but hesitating, waiting for my answer.

'Of course.' I replied feeling clumsy. I quickly took the flowers back out of the sink, so he could get to the water and seconds later I had a half-naked man in my kitchen. I had not seen him with his shirt off previously – I have to say it was a sight worth seeing. I knew he spent time in the gym and watched his diet but seeing his muscles move beneath his skin as he wet and quickly scrubbed the red marks on his shirt made me forget Brett for a moment.

My doorbell rang.

Of course, it bloody did.

Tempest looked up in question. I gave myself a mental slap. I was certain without looking that it was Brett at the door. We were going out on date number two, he was clearly just as interested in me as I was in him and here I was with a topless man in my flat and two glasses of champagne on the side. Added to this was the unavoidable fact that Tempest and Brett did not like each other.

I opened the door. Brett held a large bunch of flowers and a bottle of champagne. I could not see the label on his bottle, but I would I was willing to bet its price tag fell somewhere between really expensive and damned extortionate. The bunch of flowers was twice the size the ones Tempest had bought me.

I hadn't gotten around to telling Tempest I was going out on a date with Brett yet. I had been sort of avoiding the subject since he was being so nice and disliked Brett so much. Now though, I was stuck on my doorstep struggling to work out what my next move was.

Brett smelled wonderful, he always did. Part of me wanted to get his shirt off so I could reassure myself that he compared favourably with Tempest. I could not see how I would pull that off though.

'Err. Hi, Amanda.' Brett said still stood on the doorstep with his hands full. I had just been staring at him while I tried to work out what to do.

'Sorry. Sorry, Brett. Please come in. This is so nice of you.' I said taking the flowers and leaning in to give him a quick kiss on the lips.

'You told me you solved your first case. I felt that warranted a celebration. So, I... Ah.' Brett had come into my small flat and instantly spotted Tempest stood at the sink. With the kitchen counter in front of him, I realised that Tempest looked like he wasn't wearing anything at all and had dived behind the counter to hide.

There was a brief pause. I wanted to say something, but my mind had gone to utter jelly. I could feel the tension mount. Brett's grip on the champagne bottle was turning his knuckles white.

Tempest moved first. 'Brett, good evening.' He said extending his hand and coming around the counter to show that he was actually wearing trousers. 'I see you had the same idea. The lady will only solve her first case once.' The two men shook hands, Brett seemed very wary. If Tempest picked up on it, he was paying it no attention. 'I managed to spill on my shirt.' He said, by way of explanation as he held up the damp item.

'You were just leaving?' Brett asked, sounding surprised.

'Indeed. I just popped in, so I could congratulate Amanda in person. It looks like you two are going out for the evening, so I'll get out of the way.' With his wet shirt in his hand, he headed for the door.

'Won't be a moment.' I headed after Tempest to see him out, leaving Brett in my living room. At the door, Tempest was already letting himself out. I felt really awkward. I knew that Tempest was attracted to me, I felt some of the same about him.

'Sorry, Amanda.' He said quietly. 'I hope I have not embarrassed you. I really should have called first instead of just turning up.' He was right in that he should have called, but he was also being a friend and making things easy for me.

'Thank you, Tempest.' I replied as he went out the door. 'I'll see you at the office tomorrow.'

As I turned to go back inside, I heard old Mrs. Stone from the floor below squeal in surprise. 'Good evening.' Tempest boomed at her, probably dashing past her still half naked on the stairs.

'Sorry about that.' I said as I went back through to find Brett relaxing on my sofa.

He hit me with a smile that went straight to my stomach and made it squirm. 'No problem.' If he wanted to comment on Tempest's presence in my flat, he found the strength to keep quiet instead. His eyes were on me as I moved across the room to snag the open champagne. I had got no further than popping the cork earlier.

'Can I offer you a glass?' I asked. He was still watching me, making me feel a little nervous. It was not that he was undressing me with his eyes, more that he had a hungry look to them like maybe he wanted to pour on some toffee sauce and eat me with a spoon. I could hear Patience's voice at the back of my head telling me that I should be whipping off my clothes to show him a slutty outfit beneath.

I brought the bottle and two glasses across to my sofa, we were going out for dinner, but I imagined the restaurant would wait for us if we were late. I would not be shocked to hear that he had bought the restaurant for that matter. He stood up as I came near, took the bottle from my hand and looped a muscular arm around my waist. As he pulled me to him a zip of excitement shot through me. We were going to kiss, and I was not sure I even cared about making it to dinner anymore.

The End

Author Note:

Hi there,

If you enjoyed this book, then I will put my hand up and say that I am the one responsible for it. If you didn't like it, then it was that other guy. Since you got this far though, I shall assume you were entertained by what you read and want more.

The good news is that there is plenty more to have.

Last night I completed my thirty-seventh full-length novel and have enjoyed crafting ever single one of them. I have a lot more stories left to tell and expect to be tucked away in my log cabin for the next couple of decades as I leak crazy adventure and mystery from my brain and out through my fingers to the page.

My children get to grow up with a dad who is there to see them off to school and there to meet them when they come home again. I can take holidays when I want, and have a job so portable, I could write a chapter sitting in a café on Main Street USA in Disney World, Orlando while my kids run riot in the park. I probably won't, although if unparalleled success come my way, I might buy a beach house so I can go surfing.

Success or not isn't a big driven for me. Having a life was. But mor than that, I needed to escape the constant noise in my head as my imaginary characters demand to be set free. I have been making up stories in my head for as long as I can remember and now watch as my four-year-old son does the same.

Whatever, you are doing, and whether you decide to read more of my books or not, I wish you well.

Take care

Steve Higgs

June 2020

Extract from The Harper Files: Case 2

Last shift. Sunday, October 30th 1156hrs

I hated running. I was sure I shouldn't have to run this much as a Police Officer. Surely when I shout for a criminal to stop running, they should stop. This guy hadn't read the rules though, so he was tearing down Week Street in Maidstone with no intention of slowing down.

He was just a petty pickpocket, one of a gang that had been targeting Maidstone town centre recently, snatching purses and pilfering wallets. Or lifting people's shopping bags when they were not looking. There was almost always a crime being committed in Maidstone, it was just that kind of town where people with money mixed with those that did not and certain elements tried to even the balance.

I had been posted in plain clothes to observe and ultimately find the gang. Basically, I had been sent window shopping for the day with a side order of try to pay attention to what is going on around you. It was my very last shift with the Police. I had quit several weeks ago when I finally admitted to myself that my career was not going anywhere and after I met Tempest Michaels, a local self-employed paranormal investigator. I asked him for a job and he signed me up right then and there. Now I worked for him, but I still have a week of notice left with the Police, so I was kinda working two jobs simultaneously.

I had been sipping a salted caramel hot chocolate and telling myself that ordering it skinny meant it was really low in calories when right in front of me the dopey looking kid with the spots and the dreadlocks had walked up to pram, opened a lady's handbag and pulled out her purse. He even looked up at me as he slid it into the pocket of his dirty hoody and had the audacity to wink.

I thought he was going to try me with a chat up line until I yanked out my Police ID and shouted for him to stop.

He didn't of course. Which was how I came to now be chasing the ugly, skinny little turd down Week Street towards the river. He was faster than me, but he also had his jeans on hood style like he was a prisoner in America, so they were flapping around his backside and threatening to fall down and trip him the whole time. He probably thought it looked cool.

I yelled into my microphone, a tiny handset hidden in my sleeve, that I was chasing a suspect and needed back up in position. There were three of us working undercover today in different parts of the town centre, but it was not so big that we could not coordinate between us. Uniformed Police were also never far away in Maidstone and today two had been positioned at the top of Fremlin Walk where the confluence of roads created a hub for the town centre.

The youth had run past them almost before I could react though, certainly before I could raise a warning to anyone, so my backup was essentially backing me up now by running along behind me.

Not much help.

A cyclist came out of the cut through by Earl's pub, almost knocking the dick with the dreadlocks over. He leapt past him though as the cyclist saw him at the last moment and hit his brakes. This put the damned cyclist directly in my path and I ploughed right into him, the pair of us going down to slam into the ground. Me on top of him with his surprised face jammed between my boobs.

The uniforms leapt over the mess of bike, cyclist and plain-clothes woman cop to continue the pursuit, but the pickpocket had gained valuable yards. The likelihood of him escaping though was slim. Maidstone is too open, there are no clever alleyways to duck down that would aid his evasion. His only hope would be to pick up a bike or get into a car.

No sooner had the thought left my brain than a brand-new white Mercedes C220i AMG flew out of the gap by the Hazlitt Theatre and threw the passenger's door open. The youth was going to make it. He had too great a lead to be caught now.

Then Patience clotheslined him.

I didn't even see where she came from. I was just picking myself up and making sure my boobs were still in my top. One second, he was home free, the next his body was spinning through the air while his head rotated about Patience's right forearm.

Score one for the girls!

Patience was one of the other Officers placed in town to look for the pickpocket gang. We had been sent to different areas of the town to cover the most amount of territory, but she had been messaging me since we arrived to meet up and work together because she was bored and wanted to quiz me about my boyfriend Brett.

I apologised to the poor cyclist and got moving again.

Seeing his accomplice get taken down the driver of the Mercedes hit the gas and belted down Week Street towards the A229 where he could filter into the moving Sunday traffic and escape. He was not having a good day though. Ahead of him, the lights changed and an Argos truck swept out of Pudding Lane. With nowhere to go, I watched as the brake lights flashed on, but he slammed nose first into the side of the truck, ruining the beautiful new German car, which was probably stolen and creating a roadblock.

Patience was stood over the youth I had been chasing. I was out of breath, but there seemed to no longer be much cause to hurry, so I ambled towards her at a fast walk. Downhill from me Simon and Stephen, the two chaps in uniform caught up to the ailing car just as the driver was trying to get out. He was roughly grabbed, cuffed and forced into a sitting position by the car's rear wheel.

'Hey, butt monkey!' Patience was making her arrest. The youth was laying on the floor groaning a little and slowly writhing around in pain. 'Hey! I am arresting you for the crime of having a ridiculous haircut, crap clothes and for being a douchy little purse snatcher.' Patience didn't worry too much about doing her job properly so long as she enjoyed herself.

I arrived at her position where a small crowd was beginning to gather. Human nature dictating shoppers or people passing by were always ready for a little street theatre.

'Hey, girl.' she offered me a high five. 'Did you see the sale on at House of Fraser? I nearly spent next month's wages. They have too much fine clothing.'

'We should get this one to the station.' I said.

'The uniforms can pick him up in a minute. Patience needs some lunch.' She was staring at my chest. 'You know your boobs are lopsided right?'

I looked down. Dressing this morning for undercover work in town, it had not occurred to me to put on a sports bra. I had not figured on needing to chase anyone. I turned away from her to rearrange myself, then realised I had a three-hundred and sixty-degree crowd. My boobs were going to have to wait.

A squad car was making its way past the wreckage at the bottom of the road, being waved on by Simon. A second car was behind it and behind that a third car which would probably contain Chief Inspector Quinn. The second car peeled off to stay with the crashed Mercedes, while CI Quinn's car kept on coming up the road to where Patience and I were standing.

Both cars ground to a halt right next to us, the crowd parting only when Patience yelled at them to do so.

Three uniformed constables exited the cars, the driver of CI Quinn's car opening the rear door to let him out. I thought he was pompous and pretentious and that expecting people to open doors for him was a perfect demonstration that I was right. CI Quinn was heading to the top though and acting as if he ought to be there already was working for him. He and I had an unsteady relationship which went back about six years to when he was my Sergeant and I spurned his advances.

In a few days, it would no longer be of any concern. I did not hand my ID card back officially until November 8th, but due to overtime that I had recently put in, coupled with the holiday I had never got around to taking, I was finishing today. My uniform and all the paraphernalia that went with it was in the boot of my car ready to be handed back. I had hoped I could wrap the undercover thing up quickly enough to get back to the station and hand it all in, but alas it was already too late for that, so I would have to return tomorrow or the day after.

'Woods, report.' Instructed CI Quinn.

'Got us a dick head with a head full of dreadlocks, Chief. Woman's purse still in his possession. I think he looks like he might try to run again though. You want me to kick him in the bollocks?'

'Woods, you know how I enjoy your reports. Can you please stick to facts and not embarrass yourself perpetually?' CI Quinn replied deadpan. He was not known for his sense of humour.

'Was that a yes or a no on the bollocks?' she enquired, seeming genuinely unsure. 'A no then.' She decided, seeing his expression.

I was getting peckish. I had managed one small swig of my hot chocolate before I had to abandon it to chase Mr Dreadlocks, so now I was both hungry and thirsty and it was getting close to lunchtime.

'Do you need anything further from us here?' I asked CI Quinn directly. 'Perhaps Patience and I should return to observing the crowd in case there are more of his gang operating here?'

Ben Swanscombe was cuffing the youth and getting him to his feet.

'She hit me.' The boy protested. 'She's not allowed to hit me.'

'I stopped you is what I did. You ran into me. I was stationary, and you were moving. You can't claim I hit you if I didn't move.' Patience was well used to defending her slightly violent streak.

The youth continued to complain as he was led away and bundled into the back of the squad car.

CI Quinn was already turning to leave. 'I want you both back at the station. You have paperwork to fill out.' He ducked into his car, either to ensure we could not reply or probably just so disinterested in anything we might have to say that he had already forgotten us.

'Well, Patience is going for lunch, Chief Inspector. What do you think about that?' she said to the departing car. 'Damn that white boy sure has a stick in his arse. What do you want for lunch girl? Patience is buying?'

'You're buying? You win the lottery or something?' I wasn't saying that Patience was tight with her money, I just don't remember her ever having any.

'Girl, it's your last day. Or at least it's your last shift. Patience is going to buy you lunch.' Patience was displaying one of her rare moments of seriousness. She was a good friend. I suspected I could rely on her if I ever needed to and we had already promised to stay in touch even though we would no longer be working together every week.

'Lunch sounds good.' I answered. It really did.

'And a large glass of pinot.' She added.

'We are still on duty. We are not allowed to drink.'

'Girl, it's your last day. When are you ever going to break the rules if not now? What are they going to do to you if they catch you?'

She had a point. 'Okay, Patience. A glass of pinot.'

'Large glass.'

'Large glass.' I conceded.

'And shots.'

Lunch with Patience had not been a good idea. It had seemed like one at the time, especially when the first half glass of cool, crisp, perfect wine had wound its sensuous tendrils of relaxation into me and removed the stress I was feeling. After that took hold, I remember deciding that another glass was a great idea and my planned lunchtime skinny salad had been abandoned in favour of a pizza. Then a third glass had happened and the two of us had slunk back to the Station three hours later, armed with a quickly concocted lie about having seen some probable pickpockets and feeling the need to tail and surveil them.

No one asked us where we had been though, as if they had not even noticed we were absent. I finished my paperwork, writing up a report about the event in town, the chase, and arrest, while next to me Patience worked her way through several doughnuts she had picked up on the way back from the station because all the wine had made her hungry.

Whether I was stressed because it was my last day with a steady sensible job and the paycheck for it was about to run out, or if I was worried about my new career as a paranormal investigator, I had not been introspective enough to work out. When I talked to Patience about it, somewhere between glass two and glass three, she had said it was neither thing. In her opinion, I was getting stressed because I knew I was going to have to sleep with my perfect boyfriend soon and now I was worried that she had it right.

I had met Brett Barker about a day after I took the job at the Blue Moon Investigation Agency. He was a prime suspect in the murder of his grandfather, not least because he had inherited the Barker Steel Mill in Dartford and a sizeable fortune upon the man's death. Tempest Michaels, that's the owner of the Blue Moon business and my boss, thought Brett was guilty, and all the evidence suggested he was. I had arrested him, as I was still a serving Police Officer, but released him the next day when we determined he was innocent and he asked me on a date.

That was two weeks ago, and we had been on several dates since. I am counting him as my boyfriend already, but we haven't yet managed to get to the intimate part of our relationship. Honestly, I don't know why we haven't. There has not been a conversation where we have decided to take it slow. I am certain he is not gay, and we are both old enough to not be tiptoeing around, yet nothing beyond some passionate kissing has occurred thus far.

Patience assures me that if I do not take him to bed soon, I will lose him. Actually, that was not what Patience said. She said... never mind. Let's just say it was a more graphic version of hurry up and take him to bed.

And it was what I was planning to do. He was gorgeous. He was lean and athletic with a handsome face that smiled easily. He was an absolute gentleman and he was seriously rich. Like, buy me an island for my birthday kind of rich. We were taking it in turns to entertain each other. One date he would call the shots and take me out. Sometimes it had been swanky and expensive, like the first date when he put me on a commercial jet flying first class to Paris for an overnight stay at the Penthouse of the Ritz, but he had also taken me out for dinner in a perfectly ordinary restaurant. That we earned vastly different amounts was of no concern to him it seemed, it would only be a concern in our relationship at all if I decided it was, so I had to get over it. When it had been my turn to entertain him, I had brought him to my house for pizza, or out to the local cinema because there was a film I wanted to see. Seven dates had elapsed now though. Was that too many without some intimacy creeping in?

I had answered the question for myself days ago but had done nothing about it yet. Now it was time to fix the problem before it became one. I would call him tonight, invite him to my flat tomorrow night and shag his beautiful brains out.

The clock on the wall assured me it was nearly finishing time for me. I would have to return in a couple of days to hand back my uniform and again on November 8th to hand over my ID card. I felt no pang of separation at the thought of being without that vital piece of equipment. It was just something I had carried around with me for the last few years.

Just as I was getting out of my chair to leave my phone rang. The caller ID on the screen told me it was Jane/James calling. Jane/James is Tempest's cross-dressing office assistant. A young man that with a wig, some makeup and a dress makes a more convincing woman than I do.

'Amanda Harper.' I answered the phone. The thing with Jane/James is that he/she wants to be addressed as a boy or a girl depending on which way he/she has decided to dress that day. Over the phone one cannot tell of course, so he/she has learned to say which it is and we have learned to not assume and wait for him/her to tell us.

'Hi, Amanda. It's James.' He said. 'Are you coming to work tomorrow? We have a couple of promising cases.'

'I will be there. Just one question: Where is there now?' Two days ago, the Blue Moon office had been subjected to a firebomb and had burned to the ground. It would be rebuilt, but for now, it was very much unusable.

'Tempest has set me up in the office in his house. It feels a bit odd wandering around his house without him here, but at least we are still in business.'

'Tempest isn't there? Where is he?' I asked.

'I'll tell you about it in the morning. Or Tempest will call you I guess.' He replied.

That was cryptic. I dismissed it though. Tempest would come and go in pursuit of cases as he saw fit. He wasn't there to hold my hand and had hired me because of my ability to work independently. The pair of us might work together on cases at times but would just as often attend to separate clients.

'What are the cases?' I asked him.

'There are a few actually. The Tonbridge ghost tours are once again claiming to have a ghost that they want us to get rid of, there are some farmers out towards Cliffe that have reported mysterious crop circles coupled with odd behaviour from their cattle. However, the most pressing seems to be from a young lady that has become the target of a voodoo priest.'

'Voodoo?'

'Yes.'

'In Kent?'

'Apparently so. She met some guy on a dating website and he got a little scary and when she broke it off, he cursed her, and her hair has fallen out.'

I had picked my phone up, air-kissed Patience and headed out the door. I had to leave my car in the space behind the station as I was not at all certain I was sober enough to drive home. Fortunately, it was only a little more than a mile to my flat by the train station. I was still talking when I got outside and discovered it had started to drizzle.

Nuts.

'Are you still there, Amanda?' James asked.

'Yes, still here. Just fighting with my umbrella.' I needed both hands. 'James, I will see you at Tempest's house at nine o'clock tomorrow. Okay?'

'Sure thing.'

'I expect the cases can wait until then.' I said goodbye and disconnected. The damned umbrella catch was sticking and refusing to open. I was hovering in the doorway at the back of the station grunting and swearing. Finally, it popped, and the handbag handy brolly flung itself from closed to inside out and then mockingly refused to go back to a useable state. It learned to rue the day as I shoved its useless arse into the first trash bin I came to.

I trudged home through the increasing downpour, my hair a sodden mess on my shoulders by the time I got there. Mrs. Stone was just wheeling her bin outside when I came hurrying up the path towards outbuilding. I lived in a four-story block of flats not far from Maidstone East train station. The location was favoured by city commuters heading to London as the price of living here was far more affordable than the cost of living inside a London postcode. I was fortunate enough to have secured a flat on the top floor when they were first built five years ago. It was a small place but was still easily big enough for me and had been fitted out with good quality cupboards and appliances in the kitchen and also well-appointed in the bathroom. The rent was affordable – more so now that I was going to earn more with the switch in jobs and I saw no reason to move. A small, but insistent voice at the back of my head, that sounded suspiciously like my mother, told me I should marry Brett and move into his twenty-five-bedroom palace.

I ignored it.

I hadn't actually been to Brett's house yet as a girlfriend. The last time I was there I was tossing the place looking for evidence. I would get there soon enough but I was in no hurry to be a wife, or a mother or anything other than what I was. Mostly I struggled to look after myself, all too often discovered that I had no clean knickers to put on and regularly opened the fridge to find there was no food in it. Each time I did so I promised to organise myself better. But I never did.

'Hi, Mrs. Stone.' I called out in passing. She was wearing a pink warm-up suit and pink sparkly fake Ugg boots. Her silver hair was also dyed a shade of pink and over it all, she had on a terry dressing gown in a contrasting lemon hue.

She waved a hand in reply as she manoeuvred her bin into place by the curb ready for the morning. I made a note that I needed to do the same as they only came every other week and I had missed the last two collections.

Inside my flat, I set the bath taps to run hot water. My hair was already wet, so a bath seemed perfectly timed. I swiped my phone to connect to the speaker and pressed play. A heavy bass started thumping through my apartment as I sashayed into the bedroom to peel off my damp clothes.

I had expected to feel buoyant this evening. I need never put my uniform on again. I ought to be celebrating. Oddly though, I felt a little uncomfortable, as if I had done something wrong and was about to be exposed for it.

My phone rang. It was not a number I recognised. Ignored it rang off and I flicked the button to silent as I slipped into the bath. Ordinarily, I would have taken a glass of wine with me, but after the overindulgence this afternoon I was sipping water instead.

105

Forty-five minutes of soaking, scrubbing, exfoliating and moisturising later I was getting hungry. The pizza, eaten in a wine induced haze of false hunger was now forgotten demanding I forage for sustenance again very soon.

First though, I would call Brett. It was a call I had been planning in my head for a couple of days. I wanted to get him naked and I wanted him to know that this was my plan, but in a subtle, sexy way that would leave him hopeful, but not certain of my intentions.

I really ought not to feel nervous. I found it both exhilarating and worrying that I did. Brett Barker was very much unlike any other man I had ever met. Ignoring the bank account that equalled a small European Country's GDP he was a man that was at the same time utterly confident and yet still somehow unsure of himself. That he could nurture in me a desire to look after him while also willingly giving myself up as his sex-slave gave me a rush. He was exquisitely handsome, and I could only imagine what he would look like naked. On the few occasions when my hands had touched his arms, or torso or anything else it was clear he was lean and muscular beneath his clothing. Not like a bodybuilder, but like a well-toned athlete.

The phone was ringing at his end. 'Amanda, hi.' He even said my name like the words were caramel being spooned into my ear.

I had it bad.

'Hi, Brett. Are you free to talk?'

'Absolutely, I just got back from the gym. I am on my way to the shower, but I am in no rush and would much rather talk to you than do anything else.' He was naked! Slutty Amanda wanted to ask him to send a selfie right now. Fortunately, the sane Amanda was in charge at the moment, so I came up with a different question instead.

106

'What are you doing tomorrow night?' I specifically said tomorrow night and not tomorrow evening although I was not sure he would pick up on the subtle nuance of the words.

'Dear lady, I will be doing whatever you tell me to do.' His voice had deepened and taken on a husky tone as he spoke. It made me think that he was thinking sex thoughts. 'It is your turn to host me for a date after all.' He added his voice back to normal and full of enthusiasm.

'Well, Brett. I was hoping you would be okay to come to my flat tomorrow. I have something special planned.' I had not intended to say the word *special* so breathlessly, but I did and was certain it had left no ambiguity in my intentions for the evening.

'That...err. That sounds like an event I should not miss.' He said, stumbling but recovering well, the husky edge back. I could only imagine what my playful words were doing to his blood flow. I was already imagining the blood flowing somewhere very particular.

'Eight o'clock. Bring wine. I'll be waiting, lover.' The last word had slid out as an intended promise.

I heard him swallow at the other end of the line. He got it. 'I am... looking forward to it already, Amanda. I will see you at eight.'

'Until then, Brett.' I breathed into the phone. My God, I was aroused already thinking about him. He bid me a very good evening and was gone. Off to get a shower, possibly a cold one.

I needed to get off the bed and think about something else. Making a shopping list/list of things to do was required so I sat on the couch and got on with that. I needed to buy condoms for starters. He might well bring some but better to be prepared. I needed to have food in that was easy to prepare. I needed to get a wax and would have to fit that in around work tomorrow and I needed to clean the flat, wash and remake the bed linen and very possibly buy new underwear.

While I had been on the phone to Brett, I had received a call that I had of course ignored. Now that I looked though I saw it was the same number as earlier and I now had no fewer than five missed calls in the space of just over an hour. It seemed easier to call it, deal with the salesman on the other end and then block the number than it did to continue ignoring it, so I pressed dial and set my face to angry, so I would be ready to deal with the annoying person at the other end.

The voice though was that of a young woman. 'Tempest Michaels?' she asked hopefully.

'No. Amanda Harper. I am Tempest's business partner. Can I help you?' I hoped this was a client and not a girl he had met in a bar.

'I think he took my cat. I don't know what to do. He just won't leave me alone and the Police won't do anything.' The words had come out in a torrent, like they had been building up, threatening to overflow and were suddenly without a barrier to hold them in place.

I tried to calm her. 'Miss, I need you to slow down. Then we need to back up a little. Can you tell me your name please?' I snagged a notepad and a pen from the coffee table and sat on the sofa.

'Sorry.' Her voice was close to a sob. 'My name is Kimberly Kousins. I am being stalked by a Voodoo priest and I think he may plan to kill me.'

I switched to cop mode. 'Kimberly, where are you now?'

'At home.'

'Are you by yourself and is the house secure?'

'Yes, and yes.' She answered confidently.

'Do you believe the man will attempt to force entry? Has he displayed any behaviour so far that would suggest he is violent?'

'Not so far, no. He is very scary though.' She told me.

'Okay, Kimberly. Where is home for you?'

'Maidstone, the Mongrain Estate.' This was not welcome news. The Mongrain Estate in Maidstone is a lot like Mogadishu in Somalia – the nasty bit of it. During a particularly nasty turf war. Burning tyres, cars and random flying bullets were not uncommon. The people living there were not very nice generally, at least the ones you saw were not, the nicer ones stayed inside their houses hoping the world would end soon.

I had Kimberly give me her address and I promised to be there within the hour. As I hung up the phone, I considered calling Tempest to see if he had any advice, or had given any thought to the case, but I didn't. Part of me taking the job at his firm was me standing on my own feet and being able to operate on my own as an independent investigator. I would see him at the office in the morning where we could discuss this and other cases. In the meantime, I would interview the young woman and see if there was a case here or not.

The gauge on the dash of my mini claimed the outside temperature to be four degrees. It felt cooler than that and I had been shocked when I got outside to find my car not parked in its usual spot by the bins. A brief moment of panic that it had been stolen or had perhaps run away at the thought of going to the Mongrain Estate, seeped away to be replaced by shameful regret when I remembered that the car was still parked at the Police station more than a mile away because I had got drunk for lunch.

I tussled with the idea of calling Kimberly to tell her I could not make it until the morning, but she had been so grateful that I was coming that I could not in good conscience now do that to her. I slung my handbag over my shoulder and started speed walking through town.

My hands were frozen by the time I got to my car, making me wish I had one with a heated steering wheel. The hot air blowers warmed up a few minutes later, so I pointed them at my knuckles, trying to balance the air flow so that some of the blissfully warm air would also hit my face and body as it defrosted my fingers.

I left the town centre on the A229, sweeping up the hill towards the village of Loose, but turned off before I reached the tranquillity of that area and entered the Estate. Mongrain was such that someone controlling the budget had decided many years ago that it was cheaper to build a small Police Headquarters there than keep dispatching units from town. Even this late at night, with the temperature outside barely above freezing there were dodgy looking youths hanging out on street corners, younger kids riding their bikes and smoking cigarettes and older kids and adults hanging out in cars, probably doing drugs. They were not all male either, lots of them were girls, but girls that looked like they might mug you or knife you. And then very possibly pee on you for good measure.

I did not like that my car had been spotted the second I turned onto Mongrain Avenue. Laughably it was called an avenue still even though all the trees had long since been burned down or dug up. I wondered if maybe some of the trees had evolved due to necessity, grown legs and emigrated.

Kimberly's address placed her on the nicer side of the estate, which was to say there were fewer cars on bricks or refrigerators laying in the street outside her house. Not that she lived in a house. She had a flat in a building much like mine only nowhere near as nice. She lived at number two on the bottom floor. The curtain twitched as I got out of my car and stood looking at it, forlornly hoping it would still be there when I came out.

I hurried down the path, not willing to hang around in case I was spotted by the next gang of layabout kids. There was probably no danger to me, but dealing with them, even verbally was a task I would sooner avoid.

Inside the building's little foyer, several of the lights were out, but there was enough still working that I could read the graffiti. It was sprayed liberally on every surface like I had just walked into a breakdance club from the eighties. All that was missing was a couple of rival gangs having a dance fight and a gold-toothed DJ. Three steps led up to the first floor, a poor design given how many single mums must end up in buildings similar to this one.

The door to number two was open a crack, a slither of a face showing just above the security chain. The person inside decided I was who they were waiting for, the door closed to the sound of the chain being rattled and then opened again to reveal a woman of about twenty-five.

Kimberly Kousins was pretty but was doing her best to hide it. Despite a pronounced overbite her face was well proportioned and covered in small pimples. True to the fashion of the area though she had on a full face of makeup and crazy-long false eyelashes just to sit at home watching television. She stood five feet seven inches tall, making her quite average in height, her eyes were brown to match her hair which was pulled back into a ponytail, the length of which dictated that once released it would fall to just about touch her shoulders. It was also stuffed into a black diamanté ball cap. She wore huge gold hoop earrings which were filled with a bold letter K and were paired with no less than six more smaller hoops running up the edge of her left ear, but oddly none at all in her right. She had a nose piercing which was another gold hoop and around each wrist were colourful and sparkly Pandora bracelets. A brief pang of jealousy shot through me at seeing those particular items as I had coveted them through the shop window for many months now. I could buy them for myself but somehow that felt like cheating. I wanted a boy to buy the pretty trinkets for me, just like the wonderful advertisements on television.

Kimberly beckoned for me to hurry in. I felt no need to quicken my pace. There was no one else in sight, nor could I hear anyone, so I was sure I could cross the eight feet of foyer and get inside before a marauding horde descended upon us.

'Amanda Harper.' I said as I got close to her door. I was putting out my hand to shake, but she was only interested in getting me inside and shutting the door.

As I passed her, I readjusted my assessment of her height and gave her an extra half inch. I also gave some consideration to her weight which I estimated to be fifty-five kilos. She had on grey flannel sportswear. The uniform of the stupid Tempest had once called it. I understood his sentiment. Wearing a warm-up suit when not doing sports is completely fine, but I had interviewed people in my capacity as a Police Officer that had been wearing their favourite Sunday Best crappy grey outfit and thought they looked good.

'Please hurry.' Kimberly begged as I got inside. The door all but slammed behind me. 'I don't want Mrs. Hamilton to see you. She keeps telling the other neighbours I am a prostitute. She will think you are my social worker.'

I didn't know whether this was an insult or not. Did I dress like a social worker?

'Will my car be safe outside?' I asked.

'God, no.'

Jolly good. So glad I checked.

'Let's make this quick then, shall we?' I asked as I took myself to the front of the house where I could see out the window to my currently unmolested car outside.

I had arrived in her small galley kitchen. She had followed me in, looking pensive and holding her hands together as if she about to start wringing them.

I pulled out a notebook from my handbag and clicked my pen. 'Kimberly, please tell me why you called and how it is that you think I can help.'

'Like I said on the phone, I met a man online, on a dating website and now he is stalking me. The Police will not do anything, and I am scared.'

She was bordering on hysterical, almost in tears. I wanted to calm her down so that I could better question her. 'Kimberly, why don't you put the kettle on and make two nice cups of tea?'

'I only have coffee.'

'Coffee will be fine.' I replied, wondering what kind of person did not have the means to make a cup of tea. It was the action though, not the beverage itself that I was after. The mundanity of making a hot beverage would focus her on something else and help to re-establish a normal pulse rate. As she busied herself at the sink filling the kettle, I started asking questions.

'Kimberly, let's start with a few basic pieces of information.' I found it was better to get a person talking about facts first. It established a baseline and got them into the frame of mind for answering questions. I asked her age, her profession, where she worked, where she had grown up and noted the answers on a fresh page. I kept going with the details of her life until the coffee was made. Then switched tack. 'The man's name, what is it?'

'Bartholomew King. He calls himself the Mongrain King.'

'The Mongrain King.' I repeated as I wrote.

'Ridiculous, isn't it?' she asked, a nervous laugh escaping with the question. 'I had heard of him, or at least I had heard of the Mongrain King, but I didn't know it was him until we went on a date.'

'Explain how you met please.'

'It was online. There is a dating website called *Want some Action?* Have you heard of it?' her face coloured as she named the website. I made no comment. 'I found him on there. You can search by distance from your postcode. No point finding a guy if he is in Scotland, right?'

I indicated that I was listening and wanted her to continue.

'Well, it was me that approached him. You could say I brought this on myself. He has such a nice smile and it said he was less than a mile from me. We exchanged messages for almost two weeks and he was quite sweet. He talked about looking after his Nan at the weekends and about his job at an insurance broker in town. In the end, I had to ask him out. Ask him if he wanted to meet. I didn't think he was ever going to, so I took the lead.' She stopped to take a sip of her coffee and to shudder a little. Retelling her story was taking some effort.

'Go on.' I encouraged.

'That was three weeks ago. We met for coffee in town and he was still this really sweet guy. I liked his bald head and he has a perfect smile that made me want to take my knickers off.' I didn't write that bit down. 'I kissed him at the end of the date and we arranged to meet each other two days later. That was where it all started going wrong.'

She paused to drink more of her coffee. I did likewise but didn't get more than the first mouthful in as it was quite awful. It was instant coffee but must have been a supermarket or budget brand. I managed to swallow the foul dishwater rather than spit it back into the mug, but I was not going to have any more.

'He texted me later that evening to set up the next date but he wanted to see me the next day. I had already said that I could not because I had a Zumba class that evening. He wouldn't take no for an answer though and he said he knew how much I was into him, how much I wanted him and when I said I thought it best if we didn't see each other again he got quite angry.'

115

'Did he threaten you?'

'Not in a text message or on the dating service. The Police said that because I had no evidence to show that it was anything more than a lover's quarrel, they could do nothing about it. Not even speak with him.'

'That's right, I'm afraid.'

'What do you mean?' she asked me mystified.

'The Police have limited resources to appropriate to their workload and have to prioritise constantly. Inevitably, cases where there is no provable crime get very little attention. Stalker cases are very hard to prove and of course, they get lots of false reports each week.'

'But he cursed me.' She said with a sob, burying her head in her hands.

'What do you mean by that?' when she failed to answer after several seconds, I had to repeat the question. She still didn't answer and just as I was about to speak again, she reached up with one hand and pulled her ball cap from her head. Several pieces of her shoulder length brown hair fell out as she did so, and she met my gaze with a glum expression.

'He came to the house two days after I had met him in town for coffee. He was waiting in the bushes out the front with some of his crew and ambushed me before I could get into the house. He was naked from the waist up and he had bones painted all over his skin to make him look like a skeleton. He had a small snake in one hand and a headless chicken in the other. He flicked the chicken at me and covered me in its blood. It was so disgusting.'

I was making notes but thinking that I really didn't want to ever meet this guy.

Kimberly had more to say. 'He kept chanting the whole time. Chanting and laughing, like it was funny to him. the rest of them were laughing too. They were blocking my path in every direction.'

'Did any of them touch you?'

'No, none of them did. I screamed at them to get out of my way, but they just laughed some more and then he clicked his fingers and they all stopped. That's when he said I was cursed. That he had laid a curse upon me and I would be afflicted with ugliness for spurning him. My hair would fall out, my teeth would fall out... all that sort of thing. Then they walked away. Just walked away like it was done. I locked myself in my flat and kept expecting them to come back. But they didn't. I saw him the next day though. When I was leaving for work, he was stood on a street corner, like he was watching for me or something. He smiled and waved, but not in a friendly way.' She finished her coffee and saw that I had let mine go cold.

'Sorry, I'm not really thirsty.' I said. She didn't seem to care. She got up to put her mug in the sink. 'Kimberly, I need to fill in a few missing details. What was the date when you first made contact and when you went on the first date?'

'The first date was a Monday night, two weeks ago.'

I did some mental maths. 'The 17th?'

'If that was a Monday two weeks ago, then yes. I made first contact with him on the Saturday night before that. I am so stupid. Why the hell did I contact him?' I understood the sentiment, I had asked myself the same question about a boy before.

'So, what happened after he claimed to have cursed you?'

'Nothing. At least not for a while. It was four days later when I noticed there was more hair than usual in the shower drain. I didn't think anything about it at first but the next day there was blood on my toothbrush and even more hair in the shower. I saw him every day after that. He was always somewhere different, but it was as if he knew where I was going to be. I saw him in town on my lunch break, on my drive home, outside my window at night. When it wasn't him it was one of his awful crew of followers. By the time I gave up on hoping the Police would do something and called your investigation agency my face was breaking out into spots and my hair was coming out in clumps.' The last sentence came out between sobs. The poor girl was having a bad time of it, picked on by a gang of bullies led by a man that sounded like a real charmer. He and I would be having words in due course, but for now, I needed to wring whatever more information out of her that I could.

'Kimberly, I think I should start by ruling out the possibility that you have been cursed. Voodoo, like all supernatural legends it is nothing more than embellished stories and fantasy for the gullible. You are however the victim of some nasty stalking and, if you wish to engage the firm, I will do what I can to put an end to it.' It wasn't much of a case. I expected that once I had confronted the man, he would decide it was too much effort and find some other way to use his time.

'If voodoo is all fantasy, how do you explain my hair and my bleeding gums and loose teeth and my spots?' Kimberly was all snot and tears.

It was a good question. One for which I did not have an answer.

'I'm going to be ugly.' She wailed loudly. 'And he took my cat.'

I hated when the victims got all emotional. It was an unavoidable part of the job as a Police Officer, but I had hoped it would be a less regular event as a private investigator. Notice of bereavement, whenever I had

118

been tasked to deliver them, had been a two-person job and I had always positioned myself nearest the kitchen, so I could offer to make the tea and not be the one putting an arm around the bereaved. Here I was though with a sobbing, snot-dripping young woman and no chance of back up.

'Tell me about your cat. When did it go missing?' I asked by way of a distraction.

'He took her three days ago. At least that is when she went missing and she has never gone missing before. She is a two-year-old Persian with a blue-collar inset with Swarovski crystals.'

I jotted the information down. Given his trick with the chicken, I worried for the cat. 'Her name?'

'Miss Pussy.' She replied with a half giggle that escaped her lips between the sobs.

I wrote the name down without making comment. 'Are you sure she has not got locked in somewhere? Cat's do that.'

'No, I cannot be certain. But I would not put it past him.' Kimberly gave herself a shake.

I looked down at my notebook, I had several pages worth of jotted lines. Plenty of detail. The question now was how to approach the case. 'Kimberly, what outcome do you want to get from this?' I asked. I had learned at some point that a lot of people reporting crimes against themselves are not seeking justice, mostly they want to offload the information and never think about it again. Some though want the perpetrator behind bars and yet others want the Police, or perhaps God, or whoever is feeling most into retribution that week to deliver a broken arm or something.

119

Kimberly fixed me with an expression that suggested I was stupid. 'I want him to lift the curse, return my cat and leave me alone.' She stated with some frustration as if it were obvious.

Return her life to normal I wrote on my page and underlined it.

'Okay, Kimberly. I am going to take this case, but we need to discuss fees first.' I wondered what the girl could afford. If she had any worthwhile money tucked away, she would be spending it on moving somewhere nicer. I wondered how Tempest would feel about me taking a case at a lower fee than usual. He has often said the business cannot always be about profit and I had noticed in him a need to play the part of the hero when there was a woman in trouble.

I outlined to Kimberly our standard fees, watched her eyes widen and her bottom lip wobble again and offered her a discount. The discount came courtesy of her agreeing to help on the case where she could.

We settled on a rate that she could afford, and I explained what my likely next steps would be. I asked if she could go to stay with her mother or a sister or other relative, but her parents were away on an eight-week cruise they had saved up for to celebrate her Dad's retirement, she was an only child and had very few other relatives. I wanted her to stay in the house and thus defuse his ability to intimidate her while I gave some thought to how it was that she was losing her hair and teeth and suddenly getting spots. She would not though. She had work in the morning and refused to call in sick. I didn't say it, but I was impressed by her determination to soldier on.

I could do nothing else for her tonight. I closed my notebook, put it away and promised to call her the next day with an update. I was not going to do anything more tonight. As I thought that, a yawn forced my mouth open. I was tired. It had been a long day already which had started at six o'clock this morning with a trip to the gym.

Kimberly showed me out, her parting comment to wish me luck and to beg me to help her once more.

I left the building, walking fast to cover the distance to my car which was around the corner of the building where the car park was situated. On the bonnet of my car were two young black men.

To read In the Doodoo with Voodoo and find out what happens next, you can click this link to find it in your local Amazon marketplace.

In the Doodoo with Voodoo

Demon Bound

The Battle for Anastasia Aaronson

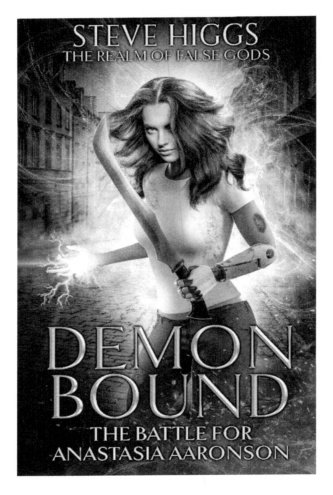

She's got a magical hand cannon and is carrying God's sword. That makes her tough to beat, but when the devil himself sends the four horsemen of the actual impending apocalypse after her …

… let's just say all bets are off.

With a demon at her side, who she's not crazy enough to trust, Anastasia is going after the missing armour of God.

It would be an easier task if anyone on Earth knew where the angels hid it.

She'll recruit help, but can she get to the armour before the horsemen get to her?

Be ready for a wild-assed ride!

A Wizard in Bremen

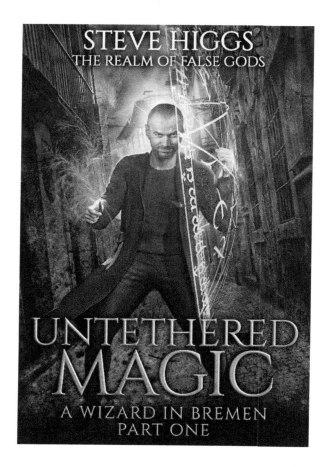

STEVE HIGGS
THE REALM OF FALSE GODS

UNTETHERED
MAGIC

A WIZARD IN BREMEN
PART ONE

When a missing persons case brings me into contact with the only other supernatural creature I have ever seen, it's not long before I am ass-deep in trouble.

The police don't like me, there's a clandestine organisation who want me to join them, and what might be a demon trying to catch me. When I refuse to play ball with any of them, my life starts to get tough, but I had no idea how low they might stoop to force my hand.

Soon they will find out just how badly they underestimated me. I hope. Have I bitten off more than I can chew?

Somehow, I need to escape captivity, cross to a mysterious demon realm, rescue a girl, and find my way back. Easy, right? It might be if they hadn't confiscated my wand.

Thankfully, I'm not alone, I have a powerful werewolf as an ally. If only he wasn't such an annoying, snarky d-bag.

More Books by Steve Higgs

Blue Moon Investigations

Paranormal Nonsense

The Phantom of Barker Mill

Amanda Harper Paranormal Detective

The Klowns of Kent

Dead Pirates of Cawsand

In the Doodoo With Voodoo

The Witches of East Malling

Crop Circles, Cows and Crazy Aliens

Whispers in the Rigging

Bloodlust Blonde – a short story

Paws of the Yeti

Under a Blue Moon – A Paranormal Detective Origin Story

Night Work

Lord Hale's Monster

The Herne Bay Howlers

The Realm of False Gods

Untethered magic

Unleashed Magic

Early Shift

Damaged but Powerful

Demon Bound

Familiar Territory

Patricia Fisher Cruise Mysteries

The Missing Sapphire of Zangrabar

The Kidnapped Bride

The Director's Cut

The Couple in Cabin 2124

Doctor Death

Murder on the Dancefloor

Mission for the Maharaja

A Sleuth and her Dachshund in Athens

The Maltese Parrot

No Place Like Home

Patricia Fisher Mystery Adventures

What Sam Knew

Solstice Goat

Recipe for Murder

A Banshee and a Bookshop

Ambassador Massacre

Albert Smith Culinary Capers

Pork Pie Pandemonium

Bakewell Tart Bludgeoning

Stilton Slaughter

Get sneak peaks, exclusive giveaways, behind the scenes content, and more. Plus, you'll be notified of Fan Pricing events when they occur and get exclusive offers from other authors because all UF writers are automatically friends.

Not only that, but you'll receive an exclusive FREE story staring Otto and Zachary and two free stories from the author's Blue Moon Investigations series.

Yes, please! Sign me up for lots of FREE stuff and bargains!

Want to follow me and keep up with what I am doing?

Facebook

Patreon